PENGUIN MODERN CLASSICS

Heroes and Villains

Angela Carter was born in Eastbourne in 1940 and later evacuated to live with her grandmother in Yorkshire. She studied English at Bristol University and published the first of her nine novels, *Shadow Dance*, in 1966. After escaping an early marriage, she used the proceeds of a Somerset Maugham Award to enable her to live in Japan for two years, a transforming experience. Her final novel, *Wise Children*, was published in 1991, a year before her death from lung cancer at the age of fifty-one. In an obituary from the *Observer*, Margaret Atwood wrote that 'She was the opposite of parochial . . . She relished life and language hugely, and revelled in the universe.'

Perhaps best known for her last two novels, *Nights at the Circus* and *Wise Children*, Carter was much admired for her work's exuberant mix of fantasy, philosophy, science fiction and satire. *Heroes and Villains*, published in 1969, is her fourth novel.

Both *The Fairy Tales of Charles Perrault* and *The Infernal Desire Machines of Doctor Hoffman* are also published in Penguin Modern Classics

Robert Coover is the author of some twenty books of fiction and plays, his most recent being *Noir* and *A Child Again*. He has been nominated for the National Book Award and awarded numerous prizes and fellowships, including the William Faulkner Award, the Rea Lifetime Achievement Award for the Short Story, and a Lannan Foundation Literary Fellowship. His plays have been produced in New York, Los Angeles, Paris, London and elsewhere. At Brown University, he teaches 'Cave Writing' (a writing workshop in immersive virtual reality), and other experimental electronic writing and mixed media workshops, and directs the International Writers Project, a freedom-to-write programme.

ANGELA CARTER

Heroes and Villains

Introduction by ROBERT COOVER

PENGUIN BOOKS

PENGUIN CLASSICS

Published by the Penguin Group
Penguin Books Ltd, 80 Strand, London WC2R 0RL, England
Penguin Group (USA) Inc., 375 Hudson Street, New York, New York 10014, USA
Penguin Group (Canada), 90 Eglinton Avenue East, Suite 700, Toronto, Ontario, Canada M4P 2Y3
(a division of Pearson Penguin Canada Inc.)
Penguin Ireland, 25 St Stephen's Green, Dublin 2, Ireland (a division of Penguin Books Ltd)
Penguin Group (Australia), 250 Camberwell Road, Camberwell, Victoria 3124, Australia
(a division of Pearson Australia Group Pty Ltd)
Penguin Books India Pvt Ltd, 11 Community Centre, Panchsheel Park, New Delhi – 110 017, India
Penguin Group (NZ), 67 Apollo Drive, Rosedale, North Shore 0632, New Zealand
(a division of Pearson New Zealand Ltd)
Penguin Books (South Africa) (Pty) Ltd, 24 Sturdee Avenue, Rosebank, Johannesburg 2196, South Africa

Penguin Books Ltd, Registered Offices: 80 Strand, London WC2R 0RL, England

www.penguin.com

First published in Great Britain by William Heinemann Ltd 1969
First published in the United States of America by Simon & Schuster, Inc. 1969
Published in Penguin Books 1981
Published in Penguin Classics 2011

002

Copyright © Angela Carter, 1969
Introduction copyright © Robert Coover, 2011
All rights reserved

The moral right of the author and introducer has been asserted

Set in 10.15/13 pt Monotype Dante
Typeset by Ellipsis Books Limited, Glasgow
Printed in England by Clays Ltd, St Ives plc

ISBN: 978-0-141-19238-3

www.greenpenguin.co.uk

Penguin Books is committed to a sustainable
future for our business, our readers and our planet.
This book is made from Forest Stewardship
Council™ certified paper.

ALWAYS LEARNING   **PEARSON**

Contents

Introduction

Like so many fairytale heroes before her, this tale's protagonist must leave home and set forth upon a perilous journey of self-discovery. After the axe murder of her beloved Professorial father, Marianne chops off her golden plaits, burns her father's books, drowns his clock in the swamp, flees her protective white tower and, in the company of her brother's killer, ventures into the dark and mysterious forest beyond the fringes of her known world. 'She loved nobody in this place but beyond it lay the end of all known things and certain desolation.' A fearsome prospect, but she is not afraid. If her savage companion claps his hand over her mouth, she bites it. 'Her ruling passion was always anger rather than fear.' This is a girl who is bored with the impotent intellectual life of the Professors, hates their community festivals and rituals, including marriage, and disdains their self-referential language – a 'severe' child who won't play the games of others, upending the little boy who, in his somewhat nasty innocence, only wants to play the hero, leaving him yowling in the dust. The boy calls her a Barbarian and a villain, and she becomes one.

In similar fashion, the author, Angela Carter, is here, in her break-through fourth novel published at the end of the turbulent 1960s, launching forth upon her own voyage of discovery, leaving behind the homey formulae of conventional British fiction and plunging into the dark entanglement, out at the edge, of 'cruel tales, tales of wonder, tales of terror, fabulous narratives that deal directly with the imagery of the unconscious'. After being labelled by reviewers a 'Gothic' writer for books she thought of as mostly mainstream naturalism, she decided, as she wrote in 1975, that she would 'indeed write a Gothic novel, a truly Gothic novel full of dread and glamour and passion. About this time, I began to read the surrealists and felt an increasing sense of justification, and what I wrote was a kind of pastiche Gothic novel called *Heroes and Villains* (after a current Beach Boys number), in which I used the framework to examine some intellectual problems about politics which were beginning to exercise me. Using an absolutely non-naturalistic formula gave me a wonderful sense of freedom.'

Like Marianne locked up in her safe but stifling steel-and-concrete tower, Carter felt penned in by the prevailing literary ideology – 'So many celebrations of the status quo,' as she called the novels of her time, mere 'etiquette manuals' – opting instead for de Sade's definition of art as 'the perpetual immoral subversion of the established order'. Writing, she believed, retained 'a singular moral function – that of provoking unease'. Opposing naturalism as a 'deeply politically repressive' propagator of dead forms and deceptive half-truths, she chose the Gothic mode, 'with its holocausts, its stereotyped characterization, its ghosts, its concentration on inner life, its rhetorical and conventionalized prose style' (all qualities present here in *Heroes and Villains*), because 'it can scarcely pretend to be an imitation of nature; so it cannot disseminate false knowledge of the world.'

In *Heroes and Villains*, the world has been devastated by a nuclear holocaust and human society has regressed to something resembling medieval Britain. Its isolated fortified villages, with their hereditary castes of Professors, Soldiers and Workers, are surrounded by dense overgrown forests inhabited by wild animals, who escaped from the pre-war zoos, and illiterate gypsy-like 'Barbarians', who live by pillage and scavenging, with subhuman mutants – 'Out People' – skulking zombie-like at the edges of the contaminated ruined cities. To save her Barbarian husband's life, Marianne has to kill one of these creatures, but feels 'neither shame nor horror, only a release from boredom and, with it, a certain sense of well-being'. Marianne is a strong-willed and independent young woman, unfazed by rape or savagery, fearing only the loss of her own autonomy, a prototype of other plucky Carter heroines to follow. Even as a child, when told that the Barbarians were cannibals who 'wrap little girls in clay ... bake them in the fire and gobble them up with salt', Marianne knows herself to be too tough to be eaten.

This clan's spiritual leader is a mad ex-Professor and magician named Donally, a giant with a forked parti-coloured beard, flamboyant costumes, teeth filed to points and an appetite for cruelty, aphorisms, myth-making and bizarre pagan rituals. Literacy empowers him among the illiterate, though he meets his match in the Professor's steely daughter. He seeks to turn Marianne into 'Our lady of the wilderness . . . The virgin of the swamp', 'Our little holy image' – 'You provide these unfortunate people with a focus for the fear and resentment they feel against their arbitrary destiny,' he tells her – but she hates 'holy images' and will have none of it. Holy images are to be unmade, not made. As her author said, 'I see my business, the nature of my work, as taking apart mythologies, in order to find out what basic, human stuff they are made of in the first place.' Carter rejected myths as 'consolatory nonsense', yet the magic of art fascinated her, and Donally is somewhat, in his crazed performances, its present caretaker. He emerges from Carter's long engagement with the medieval Merlin figure, the subject of her graduate studies; he has already turned up in *The Magic Toyshop*, in the form of the evil puppeteer Uncle Phillip, and will reach full apotheosis two years after *Heroes and Villains* as the great illusionist, Doctor Hoffman, in Carter's masterpiece, *The Infernal Desire Machines of Doctor Hoffman*.

Though Carter is yet a year or two away from the mature style that will inform her greatest work, much of what will characterize it can be found here: its fierce passion, its earthiness, its intelligence, its exuberant inventiveness, its bold rhetorical and imagistic excess. 'A linguistic dandy,' as the *Independent* called her, 'a mistress of the baroque'. Like her literary hero, Ronald Firbank, whom she declared to be 'the greatest English writer this century', she wanted a language that insisted upon itself as subject, 'a fiction that takes full cognizance of its status as non-being – that is, a fiction that remains aware that it is of its own nature, which is a different nature than human, tactile immediacy. I really do believe that a fiction absolutely self-conscious of itself as a different form of human experience than reality (that is, not a logbook of events) can help to transform reality itself.'

Robert Coover 2011

There are times when reality becomes too complex for
Oral Communication. But Legend gives it a form by
which it pervades the whole world.

Jean-Luc Godard, *Alphaville*

See how he nak'd and fierce doth stand,
Cuffing the Thunder with one hand;
While with the other he does lock,
And grapple, with the stubborn Rock;
From which he with each Wave rebounds,
Torn into Flames, and ragg'd with Wounds.
And all he saes, a Lover drest
In his own Blood does relish best.

Andrew Marvell, 'The Unfortunate Lover'

The Gothic mode is essentially a form of parody, a way
of assailing clichés by exaggerating them to the limit
of grotesqueness.

Leslie Fiedler, *Love and Death in the American Novel*

*Où fuir, dans un pays inconnu, désert, ou habité par des bêtes féroces,
et par des sauvages aussi barbares qu'elles?*

Abbé Prévost, *Manon Lescaut*

Heroes and Villains

Marianne had sharp, cold eyes and she was spiteful but her father loved her. He was a Professor of History; he owned a clock which he wound every morning and kept in the family dining-room upon a sideboard full of heirlooms of stainless steel such as dishes and cutlery. Marianne thought of the clock as her father's pet, something like her own pet rabbit, but the rabbit soon died and was handed over to the Professor of Biology to be eviscerated while the clock continued to tick inscrutably on. She therefore concluded the clock must be immortal but this did not impress her. Marianne sat at table, eating; she watched dispassionately as the hands of the clock went round but she never felt that time was passing for time was frozen around her in this secluded place where a pastoral quiet possessed everything and the busy clock carved the hours into sculptures of ice.

Marianne lived in a white tower made of steel and concrete. She looked out of her window and, in autumn, she saw a blazing hill of corn and orchards where the trees creaked with crimson apples; in spring, the fields unfurled like various flags, first brown, then green. Beyond the farmland was nothing but marshes, an indifferent acreage of tumbled stone and some distant intimations of the surrounding forest which, in certain stormy lights of late August, seemed to encroach on and menace the community though, most of the time, the villagers conspired to ignore it.

Marianne's tower stood among some other steel and concrete blocks that, surviving the blast, now functioned as barracks, museum and school, a number of wide streets of rectangular wooden houses and some stables and market gardens. The community grew corn, flax, vegetables and fruit. It tended cattle for meat and milk besides sheep for wool and chickens for eggs. It was self-supporting at the simplest level and exported its agricultural surplus in return for drugs and other medical supplies, books, ammunition, spare parts for machinery, weapons and tools. The sounds of Marianne's childhood were cries of animals and creaking of carts, crowing of cocks and the bugles of the Soldiers drilling in the barracks. In February and March, wailing gulls blew in from the sea across the freshly ploughed fields, but Marianne had never seen the sea.

She was not allowed to go outside the outer wire fence away from the community. Sheep sometimes wandered away, leaping briary hillocks above abandoned habitations, and sometimes a shepherd followed them, though he would go reluctantly and heavily armed. The Soldiers kept to the roads when they drove away lorries full of produce but, even so, the Barbarians occasionally hijacked the convoys and killed all the Soldiers.

'If you're not a good little girl, the Barbarians will eat you,' said Marianne's nurse, a Worker woman with six fingers on each hand, which puzzled Marianne for she herself had only five.

'Why?' asked Marianne.

'Because that is the nature of the Barbarians,' said her nurse. 'They wrap little girls in clay just like they do with hedgehogs, wrap them in clay, bake them in the fire and gobble them up with salt. They relish tender little girls.'

'Then I'd be too tough for them,' said Marianne truculently. But she saw the woman honestly believed what she said and wondered vaguely if it were true. She thought that at least a visit from the Barbarians would make some kind of change. The children played Soldiers and Barbarians; they made guns with their fingers and shot one another dead but the Soldiers always won. That was the rule of the game.

'The Soldiers are heroes but the Barbarians are villains,' said the son of the Professor of Mathematics aggressively. 'I'm a hero. I'll shoot you.'

'Oh, no, you won't,' said Marianne and grimaced frightfully. 'I'm not playing.'

Her uncle was the Colonel. He had a harsh, loud voice and she disliked him. Her brother was a cadet. Her mother loved her brother best. Marianne tripped up the son of the Professor of Mathematics and left him sprawling and yowling in the dust, which was not in the rules. The other children soon left her out of their games but she did not care. She was a skinny and angular child. She marked all her possessions with her name, even her toothbrush, and never lost anything.

Besides the wire netting around the boundaries of the cultivated land were the watch towers manned with machine guns stood on stilts at intervals; there was also a stout wall topped with barbed wire round the village itself. The only entry through this wall was a large wooden gate where the sentry post was. When the Barbarians attacked the community, it stood siege inside the village wall since, in order to enter the village, the Barbarians had to storm the gate. When Marianne was six years old, she saw the Barbarians for the first time.

It was the time of the May Day Festival. On May Day there was a picnic, there was music and the Soldiers performed an impressive march past and drill. Marianne's father, a gentle man constitutionally sunk in melancholy, stayed in his study with his books, such was his privilege, but her mother, the other Professor women in the tower and the Workers were very busy. They cooked succulent food and pressed best clothes. Marianne ran around bothering and pestering everybody, stealing scraps of uncooked dough and curiously indulging her spitefulness in several ways until at last her nurse said grimly: 'I'll deal with her.'

She scooped Marianne under one arm and took her to a high room nobody used. A window opened on to a little balcony of white-painted iron. She had a key to this room and she locked the door on Marianne, snapping through the keyhole: 'There you'll stay until I fetch you.' Miraculously translated from the business of the kitchens, Marianne was quite deflated. She sat on the bare boards in the middle of the floor and looked about her. A creeper wound in through the open window like a snake; there were all kinds of snakes in the forest, several of them venomous, which was not so before. Marianne was not frightened to be left alone but she was very angry. She went out on to the balcony, which squeaked beneath her feet. She peered through the iron bars at the village. It appeared diminutive, from this height, and very tidy and brightly-coloured, like a place where everyone was happy. The orchards shivered with bloom. The fields were soft green but the brambles were still pierced here and there by a few spires of steel which arched to the ground like decolourized rainbows, and leprous viaducts crested with purple loosestrife lurched towards the still uncovered core of calcined earth at the centre of the ruins. Around the edges of the horizon spread the unguessable forest.

Marianne found a piece of biscuit in her pocket and ate it. She wore a checked skirt and a brown sweater. She had long, blonde pigtails. She broke things to see what they were like inside. Her brother was sixteen, ten years older than she. Her nurse said: 'You ought to love your brother' and Marianne asked: 'Why?' Now she was left alone and forgotten, high in the tower on such a beautiful day. When she finished her biscuit, she was still hungry and gnawed the end of her plait for want of anything better.

She watched the detachment of Soldiers come out, preceded by a small military band which played a selection of marches. All wore uniforms of black leather and plastic helmets with glass visors. They had rifles slung over their backs. All the community had gathered to watch them; Marianne saw her mother and her nurse in the crowd and saw her brother among the Soldiers. Everyone was clean and proper, shirts and dresses white as paper, suits as black as ink. Marianne was bored. A bird came and perched on the balcony. It cocked its head and offered her a cynical regard. It was a seagull.

'Hello, bird,' she said. 'Have you come a long way? Have you seen any Barbarians?'

She liked the wild, quatrosyllabic lilt of the word, 'Barbarian'. Then, looking beyond the wooden fence, she saw a trace of movement in the fields beyond. It was not the wind among the young corn; or, if it was the wind among the young corn, it carried her the raucous whinny of a horse. It was too early for poppies but she saw a flare of scarlet. She ceased to watch the Soldiers; instead, she watched the movement flow to the fences and crash through them and across the tender wheat. Bursting from the undergrowth came horseman after horseman, filling the air with terrible screamings. They were dressed in furs and brilliant rags. A look-out in a watch tower had already been strangled to let them through and the men at the sentry post were playing cards so they did not see the visitors in time; two Soldiers, paying the price of lack of discipline, were shot. Then all was chaos.

The rabble came to ravage, steal, despoil, rape and, if necessary, to kill. Like hobgoblins of nightmare, their flesh was many colours and great manes of hair flew out behind them. They flashed with curious curved plates of metal dredged up from the ruins. Their horses were bizarrely caparisoned with rags, small knives, bells and chains dangling from manes and tails, and man and horse together, unholy centaurs crudely daubed with paint, looked twice as large as life. They fired long guns. Confronted with terrors of the night in the freshest hours of the morning, the gentle crowd scattered, wailing.

Marianne bemusedly saw a good deal of blood, as when animals were slaughtered, but when she raised her eyes from the battle-field of the village green, she noticed a second party of Barbarians (bristling with knives but far less gaudily painted) who jumped the wires without flamboyance and now, while the fighters were engaged, were calmly occupied in seizing sacks of flour, crocks of butter and bolts of cloth while nobody attempted to stop them. They went in and out of the houses, occasionally making threatening passes with their knives, and then she saw some Worker women seemed to be helping them. Marianne thought this was very interesting.

Soldiers and Barbarians fought hand to hand. Riderless horses seethed back and forth, screeching. Noises of gunfire and voices rose up to Marianne and she listened absorbedly. A Barbarian in a helmet of feathers decorated with the antlers of a stag appeared like a crazy sunrise on the flat roof of the museum; he held a knife between his teeth and was about to spring into the mêlée below when a bullet shattered his eyes. The knife fell from his lean lips. He inscribed a great arc on the morning as he dived forward to the ground, spouting his brains. He was the first man Marianne saw die; the second was her brother.

He rolled in the dust with a shaggy Barbarian boy armed with a knife. They threshed and wrestled, ends of fur blurring their faces, and the knife kept flashing in the sun. They were some way from the general fighting as if they had arrived beneath her viewing platform on purpose to demonstrate violence to her. The Barbarian boy's mound of black plaits and ringlets covered and uncovered them but she saw them staring at one another, both oddly startled, as if this was the last thing they expected to happen, this embrace to the kill.

Their mother had returned to the tower. Perhaps she saw them and perhaps she called out and perhaps her brother heard her voice or some distracting noise for he glanced away from his adversary, who immediately took advantage of this lost guard to stick a knife into the other's throat. Blood bubbled. The Barbarian boy dropped the knife and clasped his victim in his arms, holding him with a strange, terrible tenderness until he was still and dead. Marianne waited for somebody to shoot the Barbarian boy but nobody with a gun was available. The boy pushed the newly-made corpse against the wall and sat back on his haunches, pushing the hair out of his face. She saw he had several loops of beads around his neck and his hands were covered with rings. Since Marianne looked down at him from so high up, he appeared foreshortened and she only noticed his rings because they caught the light. The sound of the fighting was terrible music. The boy looked up and saw the severe child who watched him.

An expression of blind terror crossed his face, which was painted in stripes of black, red and white. He made some vague, terrified gestures with his hands; when she was much older and thought about him, which she came to do obsessively, she guessed these were gestures with which he hoped to ward off the evil eye. She chewed her pigtail. He scrambled upright. Many bullets now rattled into the wall behind him; a bullet struck the corpse so it shuddered with the imitation of life but a riderless horse galloped through the gunfire and the boy was all at once up and gone. The horsemen were all gone; the raid was all over.

There was now a deep silence broken only by the lowing of frightened cattle and the screams of a few dying horses and some dying men. Five Soldiers died, in all. A couple of Barbarians were left behind, too badly wounded to escape; the Soldiers briskly shot them, dug a pit and buried them. A woman had gone away with the Barbarians, as sometimes happened. Food, cloth and also some calves and chickens had been taken, enough to recompense the raiders for their losses. It was typical of any of their visits.

Her father found Marianne when it was dark. She was asleep in the farthest corner of the room from the balcony. She was sucking her thumb. She dreamed of dark, painted faces and woke in tears. Her father kissed her.

'It is all over and you must go to bed.'

She was hungry and remembered she had seen unusual amounts of food prepared that morning; she did not know these had become the funeral baked meats.

'I want cakes and stuff,' she said.

'You mustn't ask your mother for cake, now,' he said and brought her milk and slices of bread and butter in her own room. Although she did not know why, she cried herself to sleep; her father held her hand for a while. He had no hair on his head nor any eyelashes, either.

'Your brother's gone to the ruins, where the dead people go,' said Marianne's nurse. 'It's well known the ruins are full of ghosts.'

Wherever he went, their mother shortly followed him. Her son's death broke her heart; she lingered on for two more years but when she ate some poison fruit she took sick almost gladly and made no resistance to death. After that, Marianne and her father lived alone together with the old nurse, who was now too old to live anywhere else. They got on very well. He taught his daughter reading, writing and history. She read his library of old books; in the white tower, in his study, she looked out of the window across the fields to the swamps and brambles and tried to imagine a forest of men.

'Can you visualize the number "one million", Marianne?' said her father. Marianne tried to envisage all the people in the village and then that again and then that again and that again, again and again, until they were infinite, there was no counting them, and she shook her head.

'Say goodbye to the concept of plurality, in that case,' he said. 'It used to be very important. And what does the word "city" mean?'

She thought for a while.

'Ruins?' she hazarded.

So he directed her back to his books, Mumford etc., and to the dictionaries; but the dictionaries contained innumerable incomprehensible words she could only define through their use in his other books, for these words had ceased to describe facts and now stood only for ideas or memories.

She grew less spiteful but now showed unusual lines in her face as if she would not be easily satisfied. Her father said there were no such things as ghosts so she would go off by herself into the swamp, although her nurse forbade her. Marianne was very wiry and agile. She picked her way where the sheep went, trying to imagine numbers of men, women and children, but she never fell over or hurt herself. She learned to beware of the ugly plants covered with razor-sharp thorns that grew everywhere and never even to touch the sticky, green and purple berries swarming with iridescent flies which these plants produced in autumn, for the noxious sap burned the fingers. She knew how brambles sometimes masked the mouths of bottomless vents in the ground, the original purpose of which baffled her. She found out that if she ignored the obese and hugely fanged rats who nested in the choked sewers and sometimes came out to play, they would ignore her.

Shells of houses now formed a dangerous network of caves, all so overgrown it seemed nothing could ever have lived there and she never found anyone, though sometimes she would find the picked remains of bones of animals and human excrement, indicating that the ghosts in the ruins ate and defecated and therefore were unlikely to be ghosts at all, or ghosts only in the sense that they had forfeited their social personalities, like those mendicants of the swamp who sometimes came begging at the gates of the village, men and women running with sores, filth and rags scarcely covering their deformities. Sometimes the Soldiers threw bread to them and sometimes frightened them away by firing bullets over their shapeless heads but they were never let in.

'They are the outcasts of the outcasts,' said her father. When she was twelve, he told her:

'Before the war, there were places called Universities where men did nothing but read books and conduct experiments. These men had certain privileges, though mostly unstated ones: but all the same, some Professors were allowed in the deep shelters with their families, during the war, and they proved to be the only ones left who could resurrect the gone world in a gentler shape, and try to keep destruction outside, this time.'

He had read more books than any other Professor in the community. He reconstructed the past; that was his profession. His lashless eyes were bleared with shortness of sight; soon he would go blind and then have nothing but the things he could touch such as his little clock. Marianne would have to read his books aloud to him. Rousseau, for example. He was writing a book on the archaeology of social theory but maybe nobody in the community would want to read it, except Marianne, and she might not understand it. Theirs was primarily a community of farmers with the intellectual luxury of a few Professors who corresponded by the trading convoys with others of their kind in other places. And the Soldiers were there to protect them all.

'There were no wild beasts in the woods, before the war. And scarcely any woods, to speak of. And everyone alive was interlinked, though some more loosely meshed into the pattern than others. Now it has all separated out; there are genuses of men, not simply *Homo faber* any more. Now there is *Homo faber*, to which genus we belong ourselves; but also *Homo praedatrix*, *Homo silvestris* and various others. In those days, Marianne, people kept wild beasts such as lions and tigers in cages and looked at them for information. Who would have thought they would take to our climate so kindly, when the fire came and let them out?'

He was fond of posing questions of this type, as were all the Professors; but especially her father. Sometimes she thought he was not talking to her at all but to himself or to a congregation of scholars who only existed in his mind. Nevertheless, she listened to every word he said.

Now and then the community broke from its trance. A Worker went mad one midnight and fired the house where his wife and three children slept. They choked and smothered. He ran through the streets laughing and weeping, entered the Professor's tower and flung himself from the balcony. Suicide was not uncommon among Workers and Professors when they reached a certain age and felt the approach of senility and loss of wits, though it was unknown among the Soldiers, who learned discipline. But homicide was very rare and usually happened shortly before a Barbarian raid.

Another time, an old man broke into the museum and began systematically to wreck the glass cases and the treasures beneath them. He found a tin of red paint and wrote on the wall of the museum: I AM AN OLD MAN AND I WANT THE DAY OF JUDGEMENT NOW. He reached the stores of petrol with a candle in his fist but a warning bell rang and the Soldiers shot him before he could do more harm. The Soldiers also dealt inscrutably with the deformed.

Her father said: 'The Soldiers are delegated to police us and protect us but they are developing an autonomous power of their own.'

Shortly after the incident in the museum, there was another visit from the Barbarians. The raid was an expected surprise; six years was a long time to pass without one but the time-scale of the community stretched out years for ever and also somehow cancelled them out, so an event could as well have taken place yesterday or ten years before. These Barbarians were not the tribe who killed Marianne's brother; these came by foot at night, secretly and perfidiously, poisoning cattle they did not steal, sliding past the Soldiers' look-out on their bellies and strangling those on guard. Four Worker women vanished.

'They slit the bellies of the women after they've raped them and sew up cats inside,' said the nurse, now a very old woman growing strange in her ways.

'I think that's most unlikely,' said Marianne. 'In the first place, I don't think they have cats. We have cats to keep the mice from the corn and to use up our spare affection. They don't grow corn and they don't look to me as if they're very affectionate, either.'

'You young ones think you know everything about everything whereas, in fact, you know nothing about anything,' said the old woman. 'One day the Barbarians will get you and sew a cat up inside you and then you'll know, all right.'

Though Marianne did not believe her, she felt a certain quiver in her belly as though a cat, a black one like the one her nurse owned, prowled around down there. She recalled with visionary clarity the face of the murdering boy with his necklaces, rings and knife, although the memory of her brother's face was totally blurred. Sometimes she dreamed of his death; one day, waking from this dream, she realized the two faces had super-imposed themselves entirely on each other and all she saw was the boy killing himself or his double. This recurring dream disturbed her and she awoke sweating, though not precisely with fear.

'Rousseau spoke of a noble savage but this is a time of ignoble savages. Think of the savage who murdered your brother,' her father said.

'I do,' she confessed. 'Quite often.'

He wound his fingers together and looked at her with a kind of fear. He had colourless eyes, like rainwater. His voice was thin and cool and his skin had a certain transparency; he wore a good, dark suit, as all Professors did. Marianne loved him so much she only wished she could be more sure he was really there.

'Is there a young man in the community you would like to marry?' he asked her when she was sixteen.

She considered the cadets one by one. Every Professor's eldest son became a cadet among the Soldiers, that was the tradition. Then she considered the Professors' younger sons, nascent Professors themselves since it was a hereditary caste. They were all hereditary castes. She even ran her mind's eye over the Workers. After all this consideration, Marianne acknowledged it was impossible for her to consider marriage with any of the young men in the community.

'I don't want to marry,' she said. 'I don't see the point. I could maybe marry a stranger, someone from outside, but nobody here. Everybody here is so terribly boring, Father.'

'Your mother was a remarkable woman,' he said, from the depths of some sudden preoccupation of his own. 'She married me in spite of my deformity. I was a lucky man.'

'I think she was the lucky one,' said Marianne.

'We are all arbitrary children of calamity,' he said in his academic voice. 'We have to take the leavings.'

'I don't see why!' she exclaimed.

'You will,' he said. She thought of her nurse saying: 'You know nothing about anything,' and she thought: 'He's old.' She looked at him with immense tenderness, as if he were sick of an incurable disease.

'You never made friends with the other children,' he said. 'I know you'd rather not live here but there is nowhere else to go and chaos is the opposite pole of boredom, Marianne.'

They had long ago stopped using the dining-room and he moved the clock into his study. It made a small, private ticking as he talked, as if the time it told was a secret between the three of them.

'If the Barbarians inherit the earth, they will finally destroy it, they won't know what to do with it. Their grandfathers survived outside the shelters, somehow; they survived at first by accident and continue to survive only by tenacity. They hunt, maraud and prey on us for the things they need and can't make themselves and never realize we are necessary to them. When they finally destroy us, if they finally destroy us, they'll destroy their own means of living so I do not think they will destroy us. I think an equilibrium will be maintained. But the Soldiers would like to destroy them, for Soldiers need to be victorious, and if the Barbarians are destroyed, who will we then be able to blame for the bad things?'

Marianne loved him so she tactfully hid her yawn behind her hand. She loved him but he bored her.

She hated the May Day Festival. She took some food and escaped very early in the morning. She went farther into the ruins than she had ever been before. She found a passage that must once have been a wide road where she could walk with perfect ease. She penetrated to the fossilized heart of the city, a wholly mineralized terrain where nothing existed but chunks of blackish, rusty stone. Here even the briars refused to grow and pools of water from the encroaching swampland contained nothing but viscid darkness. All was silence; the rabbits did not burrow here nor the birds nest. She found a bundle of rags with putrified flesh inside and looked no further but hurried on until the swamp and brush began and the ruins merged almost imperceptibly with a shrubland of bushes and small trees, still pocked here and there with overgrown buildings. Then she entered the forest.

The trees surrounded her with vertical perspectives which obscured the flow of the hills. Here were wolves, bears, lions, phantoms and beggars but she saw nothing though she walked as softly as she could. It was long past midday and the sunlight fell in slanting rays on the trunks of the trees. She startled an antlered stag, who swished away through the undergrowth before she had a chance to see him properly; she remembered the antlers on the head of the Barbarian who fell from the museum roof and recollected that particular May Day was ten years before, exactly. Blossom covered the hawthorn bushes, the wilderness bloomed. Moon-daisies, buttercups and all manner of wild flowers hid in the foaming grass. She saw a variegated snake twined round the bough of a tree but it did not harm her, did not even stick its forked tongue out at her. Bird song and the wind in the leaves seemed not to diminish but to intensify the silence; she could hear her own blood moving through her body.

She thought she was alone until she came upon a man in a robe of black fur and many necklaces. She stepped back quickly into the bushes before he saw her. He was crouching on the ground grubbing up plants with a small spade and putting them in a basket. He was a huge man, well over six feet tall, with black hair frizzed out in a cloud down to his shoulders and a scanty, double-pointed beard dyed scarlet on one side and purple on the other. As he worked, he muttered to himself. A donkey was tethered to a tree nearby and, also tethered to a tree, was a child.

The child had a collar round his neck fastened to a chain. He was naked but for a very ragged pair of trousers. He was eating something and slobbering. He was twelve or thirteen. He was covered with a snaky, interlaced pattern of tattooing all over his chest, arms and face. Suddenly this child began to cry out and thresh around, foaming at the mouth. The man dropped his spade, went to the child and kicked him many times. The child shrieked and subsided to a babbling murmur, rubbing his ribs where the man had kicked. The man returned to his gardening without more ado, referring from time to time to a book with coloured illustrations which lay on the ground beside him. Marianne was surprised to see the book for she had been told the Barbarians were quite illiterate. The red marks of the blows glowed against the greenish pallor of the child's flesh. Marianne slipped away noiselessly. She had thought herself entirely private and was a little unnerved to unexpectedly encounter a man with a book.

She soon found herself on a road. She broke through a brake of hawthorn and tumbled down a bank on to a wide, firm, green highway – green since overgrown with grass and weeds but, still, a road. She clambered back into the hedgerow and concealed herself, for she heard the sounds of horses' hooves. She was not frightened at all, only curious; the nomads rounded a curve in the road and, from her hidey hole, she watched them pass.

They had rough, unpainted carts piled with cooking gear, blankets, skins of animals, weapons and other domestic equipment she could not identify. A few children, some of the crippled and some of the old rode on the carts but most of the women walked beside them, even those swollen with pregnancy. Many of the women were pregnant. They guided the horses or drove a few skinny cattle before them. There were many horses and ponies, far more horses than cattle or goats.

The women wore trousers or long cumbersome skirts made out of
stolen blankets, or stolen cloth, or leather, or fur. They had blouses,
some beautifully embroidered, and rough, sleeveless jackets usually of
either fur or leather; some wore Soldiers' jackets though the black
leather had been transformed by the application of beads, braiding and
feathers. They were all decorated with astonishing, tawdry jewellery,
some of it plainly salvaged from the ruins and of great age, some weirdly
fashioned from animal bones and baked clay. Their hair was wound
with ribbons and feathers; their faces were painted a little round the
eyes or else tattooed with serpentine lines like those on the child in the
wood. Most were barefoot, though some wore stolen boots or sandals
made of straw.

These women were both worn and garish. She had never seen
women like them before, so bright and wild and hung about with
children. The domestic life of the Barbarians was a mystery to her; she
had thought they would have no marriage or taking in marriage. The
outrageous visitors to her village had seemed to exist only in that lurid
moment and could have no other life, as if they were explosions of
violence produced by the earth itself. Now she saw, passing in a mute
cortège, the wives and families who profited from the looting, indeed,
who necessitated it, children too weary to cry, scabbed, dirty and marked
with malnutrition. The picture of misery.

The men walked beside them. They slouched, spat and scratched.
They, too, were hung with beads and curious stones, perhaps charms
and talismans. But they left their warpaint off though they were even
more heavily tattooed than the women. They tied back their long hair
with thongs of leather. No furs nor armour on this brilliant May Day;
most went shirtless and their bones showed through their tattooed skins.
They all had knives in their belts and most had rifles slung over their
shoulders. One man paused to urinate in the grass at the foot of the
bank where Marianne hid. There was a grisly wound on his shoulder;
he struck away flies from it, it was beginning to fester. Starved skeletons
of dogs, several with fiery eruptions of mange, walked among their
masters. Their tongues lolled out and their tails drooped between their
legs. They had all come a long way.

In the last cart of all, a very clean and stately old lady sat bolt upright. She shone like a washed star in that filthy company and she wore a prim, green dress such as Worker women wore. Her hair was done up in a knot and she wore stockings and shoes. She was obviously of some consequence in the tribe. A youngish man walked beside her, talking to her, but Marianne could not see his face because he wore a soft, wide-brimmed hat of felt pulled down over his forehead. Many of the Barbarians wore such hats. There were about sixty men, women and children in this long procession. They scarcely exchanged a word with one another, not even the children, but moved in the silence of near exhaustion.

Marianne had a clean bed and quiet sleeps. Watching these cruelly dispossessed survivors go by, she was glad she lived in the tranquil order of the Professors; she had never been glad of it before. The fearful strangers now revealed their true faces and these faces were sick, sad and worn. Two or three Soldiers could have gunned them all down as they walked and she sensed that hardly one of the Barbarians would have had the heart to draw their own weapons to defend themselves. All would fall down as if bitterly appreciative of a chance to rest. She forgave them their depredations for they had so little. Then the man on the donkey came following them with the child running beside him on the end of his chain. The man and his donkey were now hung with baskets of plants and the child's arms were full of greenstuff.

This man glanced suspiciously around him as if he guessed there were spies in the hedgerow. She shrank back among the leaves and he, too, passed by, kicking his donkey to an unwilling trot to catch up with the rest. The child blubbered with the effort of keeping up. Marianne did not know where they were all bound but she hoped it was not her home. It was a long way home.

When she finally arrived home, so late the gate was locked and she had to explain her absence to the guards, she found something had happened that wiped the Barbarians out of her mind. In a fit of senile frenzy, the old nurse had killed her father with an axe and then poisoned herself with some stuff she used for cleaning brass. The Colonel of the Soldiers, her mother's brother, took Marianne to live with him in the Barracks. She kept her father's books for a time but found she could not bear to read them and in the end she burned them. She took his clock out to a piece of swamp and drowned it. It vanished under the yielding earth, still emitting a faint tick. She found a pair of scissors and chopped off all her long, fair hair so she looked like a demented boy. She had no idea why she cropped her head; the impulse seized her. It made her very ugly and she examined her ugliness in mirrors with a violent pleasure. When she looked for the scissors again, convinced there was some other violation she could perform upon herself, she could not find them, nor could she find any knives.

'This place is like a grave,' she said to her uncle.

'There is not enough discipline,' he said. 'That old woman was maladjusted. She should have been given treatment.'

This was the way the Soldiers talked.

'She loved us when we were alive,' said Marianne without realizing what she was saying. Appalled, she corrected herself: 'I mean, when I was young.'

'She was seriously maladjusted,' said her uncle, crashing his fist upon the table. 'She should have been subjected to tests and then operated upon.'

He pierced Marianne with a shrewd, assessing glance, as if suspicious of her. He decided she should be taken out of herself.

'Learn to drive a car,' he said. 'Then you could go out with the convoys to the other communities and see a bit of life.'

He was so determined to subject her to discipline that she learned to drive. It was very easy. She meagrely survived and the Workers made the hay. It was midsummer, the air was very soft and sweet in the evenings. Just before the summer solstice, the Barbarians attacked once more, at twilight, as the lamps were being lit and the village sat down to supper. The alarm bell rang and her uncle sprang up from table, reaching for his gun belt.

'Lock the doors.'

But Marianne ran through the door while it was still open and went through the housing quarters up to a deserted dormitory. She saw the scene of ten years before, the painted Barbarians of ten years before, the tribe of the road through the forest now decked out in legendary horror. But all was obscured by the dusk, though she made out the ones who robbed quietly in an admirably ordered fashion as the battle went on; however, in the tremendous confusion of darkness, she could make out little more. Then they turned on arc lamps and the battle was suffused with white, hysterical light; but this only made confusion visible and still machine guns could not be used. Riderless horses reared like breakers in the streets. She saw a man in a dark suit rush suddenly from the tower where the Professors lived and throw himself purposefully under the hooves of a horse, which trampled him.

A blurred figure in furs materialized from the chaos. The rising moon sparkled on his necklaces. He ran down the lane beside the Barracks; she guessed he was weaponless and trying to escape. A Soldier followed him and jumped him from behind. They fell and struggled together. She was the audience again. She watched them, as she had done before, and thought she saw another death, for the Soldiers were trained in judo and karate and he brought down a chopping blow on the Barbarian's neck and left him limp in the dirt, himself returning at once to the main theatre of combat. But after a few minutes the Barbarian slowly rose and shook himself.

The lane beside the Barracks was dark and empty. The beating had clearly shaken him. He rose weakly to his hands and knees, fell down again and lay still for a while. Then he began to crawl. At the end of the lane was the shed where the armoured lorries were kept, besides a few draught horses, all in together. The Barbarian knelt on the ground, hugging his furs around him; then, supporting himself with a hand on the wall, he rose and broke into an uncertain run. He disappeared into the shed, for the door had carelessly been left open.

'We got five of the bastards, this time,' said her uncle with satisfaction. Once he had washed off the blood, they resumed the meal begun three hours previously.

'Only two wounded on our side. Look at that fool Professor of Psychology, though; kicked to death. Serve him right, maladjusted. We know their tricks by now. I did for two of them with my own hands. They were the same lot who got your brother, Marianne. I knew them by their paint. We'll send out a patrol when it's light to find their camp. Stamp 'em out. Eliminate them.'

When he reached for the bread, his hand accidentally brushed against

Marianne's and she started violently. She was perverse and she turned against her own people when she thought of the miserable encampment where verminous children and women with feathers in their hair would wait a long time for men who would never return. Washed and naked, gashed with wounds, five corpses waited for the anonymous pit; a sixth man, as good as dead, skulked in the garage. She felt an extraordinary curiosity about him. Some at least of this curiosity sprang from a simple desire to fraternize with the enemy because she felt so little attached to her alleged friends; some of it was a simple desire to see the stranger's face close at hand; and some was perhaps related to pity.

When the family slept, she took a loaf and some cheese from the kitchen and crept out into the night. They had locked the shed door securely, presumably after cursorily searching the shed, but she guessed the Barbarian was still inside it for, if they had found him, her uncle would have been sure to mention it. She knew where the keys were kept. A horse moved in odorous confinement. Hay rustled. A finger of moonlight rested on the lacquered side of a lorry. She listened but could hear nobody breathing. She spoke into the darkness.

'I've brought you some food.'

Nothing stirred.

'It's all right,' she said. 'I won't give you away.'

She stepped inside the shed. As she knew would happen, the Barbarian put his hand on her mouth and twisted her arms up behind her. She felt the innumerable rings he wore grind into her face and she immediately bit his fingers as hard as she could. He tightened his hold. He put his mouth against her ear.

'Get me out of here and I'll do you no harm but if you shout, I'll strangle you.'

His right hand dropped from her mouth to her throat; she coughed and spat.

'It's quite unnecessary to strangle me,' she whispered angrily. 'Are you hurt?'

'I fainted,' he said as if this had surprised and affronted him. He slurred his words together and his voice had the rough edges of a man accustomed to speaking in the open air but she understood him quite well. She gave him the food and he ate it. She could not see him at all.

'Will you rape me and sew a cat up inside me?' she inquired, remembering her nurse's warning.

'There are no cats to be had,' he pointed out in as reasonable a voice as she could desire. Then he resumed such an absolute silence that she told him the thing that was on her mind, as if it would explain and justify her unexpected presence beside him.

'My father's dead.'

'So's mine. When did yours die?'

'Last month.'

'Mine died this time ten years ago. He was murdered.'

'So was mine.'

'It's the same everywhere you look, it's red in tooth and claw. Do you want to come with me?'

'Yes,' she said immediately. If she had allowed herself to think, she would never have said this.

'Can you drive these things?'

'Oh, yes.'

'Then you can crash a lorry through the gate, can't you. That will be impressive.'

'I suppose so,' she said for there was nothing but custom to keep her in the village and nothing she wanted to take away with her; not a single one of all those things she had once possessively marked with her name now seemed to belong to her. She had wanted to rescue him but found she was accepting his offer to rescue her. A movement indicated his presence; she felt his hand smear some greasy thing on her face, some of his warpaint.

'I've made my mark on you,' he said. 'Now you're my hostage.'

'Not at all!' she exclaimed. 'I –'

'Open the door wide. Come on.'

In the moonlight, she was surprised by the angel of death. She was not prepared for this spectre; talking to him, she had altogether forgotten what he would look like. She scrambled from the cabin of the lorry and dashed back into the depths of the shed, looking for a place to hide from him, but he caught her easily, scooped her up and carried her bodily to the lorry, depositing her in the cab. She kicked and scratched but even now did not cry out to wake the village.

'No second thoughts, my ducks,' he said. 'You've done it.'

He was laughing and seemed very excited, as though it would have been boring and easy for him had she been too compliant. Danger was perhaps his element. He planted her hands on the steering wheel for her.

'Drive,' he suggested.

Moonlight flooded the shed and bleached the strange colours from his face but for the black that ringed his eyes, and moonlight also changed some blood on his face from red to black. The sleeping village lay under the moon; the Soldiers with their glass faces stood by the gate, glass faces even more unnatural than paint and not half so mysterious. She loved nobody in this place but beyond it lay the end of all known things and certain desolation. She hesitated and the stranger caught her by the throat again. She pushed him away and started up the lorry.

He crowed with delighted laughter.

They had gone a hundred yards before she heard the alarum bells ringing above the sound of the engine. As they crashed through the wooden gate, the first bullets from the sentries bounced off the cabin. They left the start of hubbub behind them and roared along the road the Soldiers used.

'Shake 'em off,' he ordered, hanging out of the window to look after him. 'They're coming after us on their motorbikes.'

She veered off through a field of tender young wheat. He fell back inside the cabin. The cut on his face had opened up again and he wiped away the blood with his wrist.

'Even so, it hurts me to destroy good bread,' she said.

He looked at the cornfield and then at her.

'I see you're an intellectual,' he remarked obscurely.

'I never thought you'd know such a word!' she exclaimed, tearing open a hedge.

'I'm bloody well educated,' he said. 'And my name is Jewel.'

'Who'd have thought it.'

'I am the cleverest of all the savages,' he told her. 'But by no means the kindest.'

'Will you be kind to me?'

'I very much doubt it.'

They reached the end of the farmland and went through the wire fence, setting off a carillon of alarum bells.

'I know a road through the ruins,' she said. 'Though they say the ruins are full of ghosts.'

She thought he was bound to be superstitious but all he said was:

'Drive on.'

Now they entered the arid zone and the lamps of the lorry picked out a few bony skeletons on either side of the shadow of a road along which they hurtled at a crazy speed. He stared out of the window.

'Faster.'

'I can't go any faster. Is anyone following?'

He opened the door and swung out on it; she was already growing accustomed to his extraordinary appearance, streaked with moonlight.

'Can't see. Faster, go faster, anyway.'

'I can't.'

He howled in fury and hit her. She then became very angry herself but found she could force still more perilous speed from the lorry and so they went on. The ruins dipped and reared on either side. They could not tell where their pursuers were or if they had any pursuers. The moon veered back and forth across the sky and everything around them shifted and tilted continually. Every minute she expected to crash. The forest started. To the right of the road he saw an oak tree with a thick trunk covered with ivy.

'Drive into that. Go on.'

She directed the lorry towards the tree, convinced they would both die in a few seconds. But he opened the door on his side of the cabin, grabbed her shoulders, hauled her from her seat and jumped. The lorry crashed on, driverless, hit the tree with the loudest bang she had ever heard and burst into flames. They fell softly into a marshy pool.

He released her and watched the fire. First his face expressed a delighted glee and then became impassive. The heat of the flames bathed their faces. When the green tree took fire, spurts of acrid smoke, blown on the wind, made her eyes water.

'They'll see you,' she said. 'You've sent them up a big signal to show where you are. Why on earth have you done that?'

He turned to look at her curiously. He had red paint on his cheek-bones, the firelight turned it red again. He appeared about to speak but thought better of it, shrugging.

He dragged her out of the mud and led her some distance into the forest, till they reached a place where they could see the road from the rasping core of a clump of ferns. Soon a posse of Soldiers whined up on motorcycles. Jewel clasped her mouth firmly with his hand but she would have stayed silent, anyway, for the moonlight glistened so strangely on the glass visors and slick leather limbs of the Soldiers they seemed mechanical, ingenious objects who would not have heard her if she had cried. The Soldiers searched in the glowing debris of the lorry for bones and ashes of flesh and diligently investigated the road by the light of torches they brought with them but they found nothing. They must have decided, at last, that the fire had consumed the driver along with the lorry for they gathered together, consulted for a moment, then remounted their motorcycles and drove back in a convoy the way they had come. And that was the last Marianne saw of them.

She did not know how they had described the situation to themselves, whether or not they thought it the act of a man unhinged by the day's violence; no doubt, next morning, when they found her bed empty, her uncle would murmur how she had never adjusted to her father's death, that she lacked discipline and he wished he had not taught her to drive. Then she realized with surprise that Jewel had organized an official suicide for her. He relaxed his grip. He had bruised her jaw. He was grinning; she saw his teeth flash.

'I told you I was clever,' he said. Then, as if overcome with weariness, he lay down in the grass beside her and was immediately asleep.

It grew very cold and soon the moon went down. No sound broke the dark, enormous silence of the night. She stripped off Jewel's fur and wrapped herself in it; it was the pelt of a red fox and, beneath it, he wore a rough coat of tanned hide with the pile on the inside. This coat smelled rank because the hide had been badly cured. He muttered something in his sleep and moved close to her until he slept with his head on her lap. She touched his beads and wondered whether to strangle him with them. He was very warm and very heavy; he appeared to trust her entirely and she let go of his necklace, for nobody had trusted her since her father died. They had hidden knives and scissors from her and talked to her in soft, conciliatory voices. After a while, she began to cry for her father. She could not stop crying until the day was about to begin.

Twined in this fortuitous embrace, Jewel and Marianne lay among the curling ferns. At first, outlines but no colours appeared in the forest and all was blank forms of uniform and phantom grey but, after the sun penetrated the branches, the trees acquired flesh from the darkness and, as the sky grew light, she saw nothing that was not green or else covered with flowers. Plants she could not name thrust luscious spires towards her hands; great chestnuts fantastically turreted with greenish bloom arched above her head; the curded white blossom of hawthorn closed every surrounding perspective and a running tangle of little roses went in and out, this way and that way, through the leafy undergrowth. These roses opened flat as plates and from them drifted the faintest and most tremulous of scents, like that of apples. Though this scent was so fragile, still it seemed the real breath of a wholly new and vegetable world, a world as unknown and mysterious to Marianne as the depths of the sea; or the body of the young man who slept, it would seem, sweetly, in her lap. An awakened bird clattered upwards and she heard stirrings in the brambles. Without any fear, she waited for a red-eyed wolf or grinning bear who might come, as she had heard they did, to eat up hungrily both her and her companion. But nothing appeared. Only the trees moved and they infrequently.

Meanwhile, in the village, they would be rising and making fires, smoke starting to drift from the chimneys. Women whose eyes were still thick with sleep stirred the porridge and cows lowed to be milked. Children were running to feed the chickens and the stentorian cocks didactically announced the beginning of a new day, though this new day was bound to be indistinguishable from all the rest. Except a Professor girl had gone crazy in the night and ended it by burning herself alive. As the new day began, Jewel opened his eyes and stared at her. Trapped in his regard so closely and suddenly, she briefly experienced a sensation of falling. His eyes were such a blank, inexpressive brown the colour might have been painted on the backs of the irises. The left eye was very much puffed and swollen because of the cut immediately above it. A few birds began to sing. Jewel was seized with a violent fit of coughing; his body shook convulsively, he rolled away with unexpected gentility and spat. Maybe something was wrong with his lungs. When he recovered himself, he said:

'You been awake all night?'

She nodded.

'That's pretty stupid,' he said. He looked at her closely. 'Been crying?'

She nodded again. He shrugged. The early light was now beautifully iridescent and took substantial form in drops of white dew strung out on the rough surfaces of his coat. His face was a spoiled palette; she could make out no features beneath the thick crust of colours and dried blood.

'I could have killed you in your sleep,' she said.

'But you forbore,' he remarked and was once more convulsed, doubled up with such noisy coughing he frightened morning birds into the air. When the coughing was over, he gave the impression of assembling himself together again, perhaps rather painfully, as if each attack disintegrated him a little more. But there was still nothing at all she could see of his face and what was she to do when it was so hard to look at him, harder still to describe him and hardest of all to know how he would look when they reached their destination, this wild man who now rose, stretched, squinted, first towards the sky, then downwards to the ashes of the lorry and the tree? He laughed quietly to himself. He was as complete a stranger as she could wish to meet and her only companion. He had a ring on every finger and two on some.

'Thought you was a boy at first,' he offered conversationally. 'Who chopped all your hair off?'

'Nobody. I did. Myself.'

'Thought it might be a punishment for something.' He yawned again and then approached her sideways with circumspection, although offering her his hand. She continued to sit quite still.

'What if I say I'm not coming any farther with you?'

'Well . . .' he said. 'I wouldn't believe you.'

'Why is that?'

'You can't go back to your village, can you? You wouldn't half look a fool, wandering back with some concocted story to explain what happened. And they wouldn't believe you; they'd invent a crime and punish you for it, for they wouldn't understand why you had wanted to go away in the first place and would suspect you. And you can't stay right here 'cos you've got nothing to eat and there's peril of Out People, isn't there, to say nothing of savage beasts.'

She was very affronted at this apparent cheerfulness, especially since she decided he was right; she could not or would not return where she came from nor could she stay where she was. She refused his hand and got to her feet herself. She picked up the fox fur.

'If I come with you, remember I'm coming of my own free will.'

'Oh, yeah. Sure.'

They at once turned their backs on the road. He led her through the skirts of the forest until they came to a stream. It was now fully morning and solid gold kingcups floated on the surface of the blue water. He knelt, drank, dipped his face and washed away the rime of red, black and white. She knelt beside him, bathed her eyes, wiped the mark from her forehead and also drank. She was surprised to see his real face, which was wary, withdrawn, private, full of bones, dark and scored by weather. He was clean-shaven. His ears were pierced and he wore dangling earrings made of beaten tin. He began to unfasten his braided, decorated hair.

'Why do you do your hair up so strangely?' she asked.

'It makes us more frightening,' he said and grinned. She was glad he did not file his teeth to a point as was the fashion of many Barbarians. A maze of midges began to dance above the surface of the stream.

'Is that why you paint your faces, also?'

'Sure.'

'The Professors think you have reverted to beasthood,' she said censoriously. 'You are a perfect illustration of the breakdown of social interaction and the death of social systems.'

'You don't say,' he remarked with complete disinterest. He was occupied in watching her. If he looked strange to her, she seemed at least as strange again to him, since she was so small, clean, trim, pale and sure of herself. He had never seen a woman of her class so close before and he scrutinized her curiously, taking in her cloth skirt and white blouse now daubed with mud. They examined one another like interesting specimens but he got bored with looking first. There were stories among the Barbarians that Professor women did not bleed when you cut them; however, he did not believe these stories, though he fingered his last remaining knife thoughtfully.

Soon it grew too hot for the fox pelt and she carried it over her arm. He walked on before her. Though the cloth of his clothes had been stolen from the Professors, it had been dyed from its original sober grey to camouflage colours of mossy greens and browns, for the Barbarians were hunters and practised dissimulation in the woods. He rarely glanced behind him and she had to make her way as best she could through the bushes, tall grass, bracken and flowers. She wondered how he came to be called Jewel; it was perhaps a corruption of some other name, perhaps a Biblical name such as Joel. Many of the Barbarians had adopted apocalyptic religious sects after the war, as had some of the Professors. Or perhaps he was called Jewel because he was so beautiful, though also very strange.

There were small, pink blossoms on the brambles and yellow points on the gorse. The tallest cow parsley rose five or six feet high and he often used his knife to cut them a path. Some of the stems of fern were as thick as her wrist. Tangled in briars, she called out to the young man but he did not hear her for the forest seemed to merge into an element heavier than air, which drowned her voice. And an extraordinary silence reigned. The light, filtered through the leaves, seemed perfectly green. She tore her skirt free. Jewel waited for her beneath some giant skeletal candelabra of cow parsley; he was grinning again.

'No wonder they had to put the Professors in shelters, when they can't even find their way through a wood. If I wasn't with you you'd walk round and round in circles.'

'I'm not familiar with the country,' she snapped angrily. He appeared to take immense, if derisive, pleasure in the pure, round sound of her vowels. She guessed he was taking her home as a battle trophy, of less use but more interest than a bolt of cloth. Her head ached with the viridian dazzle of the sunlit forest. As they went on, her eyes began to play her tricks. Now he seemed taller than the tallest of the trees; when he stretched out his arm, he could pull down the sky on everything. Then he shrank to a point of nothing and she lost him in the grass.

'You should have had some sleep,' he said with vague irritation, looming beside her, the whites of his eyes showing. 'Now you're all weak and feeble.'

'I shall survive,' she said, for she would not ask for any assistance.

A squirrel chattered in the branches. It ticked away like her father's clock but was a biological timepiece of flesh and blood which did not tell the hours. Turned up towards the invisible squirrel, her face looked so pinched and ghost-like that her companion suddenly doubted she was real and put his hand against her face to see if it was flesh.

'Don't touch me,' she said, flinching.

'It's no pleasure,' he replied sharply for the gesture had betrayed him; he thought he did not believe in ghosts.

Towards midday, he allowed her to rest in a clearing among some fallen stones, once a cottage. A few garden flowers wildly and unnaturally returned to nature scrambled about the fallen masonry, where trees of dark ivy grew. Outside the communities, the order of nature was awry; a bee buzzed above a magic sunflower fully two feet across. A patch of rhubarb had become a plantation of huge, sappy stems holding up a thick roof of worm-eaten leaves.

'Did they ever teach you medicine?'

'Only a little history and social theory.'

'That won't help my brother, then, who's ill.'

'What is he ill with?'

'Gangrene.'

She remembered the festering wound on the shoulder of the Barbarian she had seen on the road on May Day; gangrene would have crept over him like ivy.

'Probably be dead before we get back, anyway. My middle brother, that is. Or was. To be exact, my half-brother. All my brothers are half-brothers, see, owing to my father's wives having this facility for dying in childbirth. Have you any brothers?'

'I used to have one but the Barbarians killed him.'

'An eye for an eye, a tooth for a tooth,' said Jewel philosophically, chewing on a stem of grass.

He talked like a half-educated man and this surprised her very much since she had thought the Barbarians possessed no education at all. He also possessed, in his curiously elegant if abrupt movements as much as in his speech, a quality her father had called irony, unusual among the Professors. But, all the same, she recognized it. Talking to her, he half turned away his face and watched her from the corners of his eyes as if assessing his effect on her, or perhaps he was afraid to let her out of his sight while he was also afraid to look at her too closely. Yet he seemed to find some desperate humour in his own suspicions for she was only a young girl.

'What sicknesses do Barbarians get?'

'Barbarian . . .' he repeated lovingly, giving each syllable an equal weight so that the word lost all its meaning and became abstract. 'We get fevers from bad water. Cancers, when you grow old, if not before, or if you grow old, that is. Tetanus if you cut yourself. And that withering of the blood, you know? When you dry up and blow away in a matter of weeks.'

'Do Barbarians go mad?'

He darted her a glance of extreme curiosity.

'You don't usually get the time; you need a bit of leisure to go properly mad. Donally is mad, though. Not that I've got much to compare him with, but I think he's a bit mad, taking all in all.'

'Who is Donally?'

'My tutor,' he said. 'Dr Donally. Not that he'd teach me to read.'

'How extraordinary you should have a tutor.'

'He appointed hisself, I didn't want him. He came with a snake in a box when my father, poor old sod, was old and ill. And the Doctor came riding on a donkey and he had a baby with him, he wrapped it in a blanket and it did nothing but dribble. And he had cases of books and a whole lot of needles, for the tattooing. And colours, he brought with him, a whole lot of colours.'

'Is he a big man, with a beard in red and purple?'

'Where did you see him?' he asked sharply.

'In the forest. I was out by myself and saw your tribe ride by but I don't think I saw you. I think I'd remember you. Though perhaps not.'

'And I thought we went so secret and all.'

'I was by myself, nobody knew where I was and I didn't tell anybody. It was the day my father died and I saw your tribe. I felt so sorry for them, they were so tired. If I hadn't seen them, so defenceless, I would have told my uncle I saw you hiding in the shed and my uncle would have shot you.'

She paused, to observe his reaction, and realized she was boring him. It was about noon. The sun was directly overhead and cast no shadows.

'Come on, let's get on.'

She did not look where she was going and trod on an adder basking on the warm stone; the adder stung her calf and slid off into the bracken as quick as variegated lightning. She felt a burning pain around the wound.

'Yeah,' said Jewel with deep satisfaction, as if he had expected this.

He made her lie down on the grass, took his sharp knife and cut the wound then put his mouth against it, sucked out the poison, spat and continued to suck. She clenched and unclenched her fists to feel the extraordinary sensation of his wet mouth against her skin and the pain was terrible. It was the most primitive kind of first-aid for snakebite and she was not at all sure it would do any good. He tore off the sleeve of his shirt and bound up her leg tightly.

'Why don't you cry when you're hurt?' he said.

'I only cry out of sentiment,' she said. Nothing half so painful had ever happened to her.

'Lie still for a bit but then you'll have to walk. Or else I could leave you.' Although he was not superstitious, he was interested and perhaps relieved to see the blood on the blade of his knife.

'Oh, no, you won't leave me. Even if you have to carry me.'

'There's a change of tune, already. Lucky it was only an adder. *Viperus berus*,' he added idly. The pain made her light-headed; she did not believe she had heard him give the snake its zoological name. 'He's a poisonous snake but others are more poisonous, though I understand this was not so before; and now it's the cats, really, that are worst of all.'

'I thought Barbarians had uses for cats.'

'Who told you that one, about sewing cats inside women?'

'My nurse. But she was a silly old woman.'

'Cats and Out People are the worst, worse than wolves. Cats drop down from the boughs if you startle a den; they drop on your shoulders and rip you and rip your eyes, if they get the chance. My brother got his arm ripped. Then it festers. Some muck in their saliva, cats. They used to sit by firesides and purr, didn't they, they was well known for that.'

'All cats did that before the war,' she said. 'Now only Professor cats know their place. My nurse had a nice cat. It was black and all it did was catch mice and the occasional bird.'

'You said she was a silly old woman; it was just biding its time.'

'It was a house cat.'

'Out People, however, have poison arrows, leprosy, pox and no sense of pride, which is terrible. How does your leg feel?'

'Burning.'

'Are you scared of dying?'

'What, you mean generally?'

'No,' he said. 'This minute.'

'Not until you mentioned it. Then I felt a pang.'

'Good, I got the venom out, then,' he said, pleased. 'It's a bad symptom, it's fatal, fear of death. And you've gone white, at that.'

'Is that good or bad?'

'Good. Otherwise you've have gone all the colours of the sunset and come up in blisters, too.'

The rest of the journey to the encampment had the quality of a hallucination; now not only her eyes deceived her but also her ears and sense of balance. Sometimes he would support her, sometimes leave her to seek out a path; they came to a wide clearing full of buttercups and he left her alone with the wind which blew in her face like dishevelled hair. The surface of the meadow was restless and glittered with the motion of the grass and Jewel walked through the painted buttercups like a palpable shadow. A crow turned white as it flew through the sunshine. She was in great pain. It seemed to her that sometimes he carried her but she may have been dreaming. He gave her some brown and white honeysuckle to smell, to distract her. Under the trees, they trod a labyrinth of light and shade.

'Let me tell you a bit more about *Viperus berus*,' he said or might have said. 'The Doctor is a practical man and believes religion is a social necessity. We discuss this topic endlessly for I don't believe in it at all but I always let him win in the end for he has his poison chest, see, and I'm cautious of his poisons. So he keeps *Viperus berus* in a box out of social necessity and now and then he persuades them all to worship it.'

'Is it a phallic cult?' she asked, or perhaps asked.

'He hasn't decided,' replied Jewel, who now carried her in his arms. 'Sometimes it's phallic and sometimes it isn't, depending on his mood.'

The next thing she knew, she was limping beside him, leaning heavily on his arm and the sun had moved across the sky so the beams came down with a sideways slant. She fixed her eyes above the leaves and the thousand repetitions of green forms around her, and saw the fine meshes that dapple the sky as if they were a kind of wire netting and all underneath in a huge enclosure.

'And if you've got to worship something, why not the snake, which sloughs off its skin and turns up all fresh and ready for anything and can also form itself into a perfect circle by putting its tail in its mouth. And lives on air and soil. And carries poison in its mouth all the time, ready to defend itself. I've nothing against snakes, mind.'

'I wish I could agree with you.'

'Once bitten, twice shy,' he said.

As her nurse said to her in the kitchen when she pulled the cat's tail and the cat scratched her. Since it was a domestic cat, the scratch did not fester. She touched Jewel's earring with her finger and made it jangle like a tinny peal of bells. They might have passed a charred circle where the Out People had lit a fire and might have passed a skeleton. Then she saw a woman in dun-coloured clothes gathering fungus. Jewel motioned Marianne to keep quiet and crept up on the woman from behind; she thought he might garotte the woman, whose scream re-echoed in the ragged rooftop of the trees, but Jewel was laughing. Dropping her mushrooms, the woman fell on her knees in front of Jewel, moaning.

'Here, you didn't think they'd really kill me, did you?' he snapped at her crossly. 'Think I'm dead, do you?'

He opened the woman's screwed up eyes with his fingers and abruptly stuck his hand into her mouth.

'Taste me. I'm real.'

The woman sucked his fingers greedily and began to laugh.

'The Doctor is praying for your soul,' she said. 'When they came back without you, he said you were dead, like the others.'

Marianne found the woman's speech far more clotted and impenetrable than Jewel's; she seemed to swallow half her words before she spoke them. Jewel put his hands under the woman's armpits, stood her on her feet and led her to Marianne. The woman wore the skull of a stoat on a plaited thong of leather round her neck and her bare feet had grown a thick, protective shell of horny skin. She wore baggy trousers, a shirt with some kind of feather embroidery on it and a waistcoat of fur; she was brown with dirt. Seeing Marianne, her eyes opened wide with fear.

'This is the daughter of my father's sister's daughter,' said Jewel. The woman's eyes were open so wide Marianne could see a rim of white all round the irises. She hung back and would perhaps have run away if Jewel had not got such tight hold of her hand. She was ageless with travel and child-bearing.

'This is a girl called Marianne, she's the daughter of a Professor of History,' said Jewel. 'She knows which way time runs and came with me of her own free will. A snake bit her but she didn't die, she walked on.'

His face and voice were equally inscrutable. The woman looked from Jewel to Marianne and received no comfort from either of them; Marianne was in too much pain and far too perverse to smile. Then the woman sank down again, shuddering, and made certain gestures of the hand Marianne had first seen when she was six years old and realized were intended to ward off the evil eye. Marianne wanted to tell the woman not to be so silly but was all at once too sick and dizzy.

'Take my hand,' she said to Jewel. 'I'm fainting.'

He obeyed her.

'Please get up,' she said to the woman. 'You make me so embarrassed.'

'That's a word we woodsmen don't often hear,' remarked Jewel. 'Here, Annie, you heard her. Get up.'

He yawned, as if suddenly excessively bored. His cousin got up but she would not walk beside them; she loitered a few paces in the rear and muttered, apparently, spells and incantations. The trees thinned out and the wood ended abruptly. Marianne smelled a sharp stench of excrement and horses and they arrived.

Before her, she saw a beautiful valley of lush pasturage around a wide river hemmed with flowering reeds. On the other bank of this river from the place where they left the wood there lay a house of a kind Marianne had never seen before, though she had seen enough photographs and engravings to identify portions of the house's anatomy and give them their historical names. This house was a gigantic memory of rotten stone, a compilation of innumerable forgotten styles now given some green unity by the devouring web of creeper, fur of moss and fungoid growth of rot. Wholly abandoned to decay, baroque stonework of the late Jacobean period, Gothic turrets murmurous with birds and pathetic elegance of Palladian pillared façades weathered indiscriminately together towards irreducible rubble. The forest perched upon the tumbled roofs in the shapes of yellow and purple weeds rooted in the gapped tiles, besides a few small trees and bushes. The windows gaped or sprouted internal foliage, as if the forest were as well already camped inside, there gathering strength for a green eruption which would one day burst the walls sky high back to nature. A horse or two grazed upon a terrace built in some kind of florid English Renaissance style. Upon the balustrade of this terrace were many pocked and armless statues in robes, or nude and garlanded. These looked like the petrified survivors of a malign *fête champêtre* ended long ago, in catastrophe.

Underneath the terrace was a brilliant clump of rose trees, once a formal garden. All the roses were blossoming on tall, thorny trees which knotted together and shook down petals. Everywhere she looked were men, women, children and horses. A few half-naked children sat on the banks of the river and fished. Mangy dogs scavenged in an enormous midden of bones and liquid dung which spread out from the side of the house like a huge stain. They picked their way down the sides of the valley. A boy was breaking in a colt beside a pile of sticks. When he saw the three figures on the other side of the river, he let out a great whoop. The colt bucked and he fell off.

'That's my brother,' said Jewel. 'That's the youngest. That's the prettiest, he's precious.'

A dam in his heart must have broken with relief and joy for she saw
he was crying. The boy plunged through the waters, coming to meet
him. The children dropped their fishing rods and some ran into the
house to fetch their parents but others threw themselves into the water
to cross the river straight away. It seemed the whole camp was coming
to meet Jewel, leaving every task, running as fast as their feet could carry
them but the youngest brother arrived first and embraced the eldest,
kissing his mouth, cheek, and eyes.

'Precious,' said Jewel. 'My precious.' Not for some time did Marianne
realize that Precious was the boy's name; the Barbarians used whatever
forenames they found lying about, as long as they glittered and shone
and attracted them.

All around her she saw the behaviour of the woman in the wood
repeated over and over again. First, they looked at Jewel with trepidation,
in case he was really dead but had returned all the same, and then they
saw he left footprints in the ground and was substantial and kissed his
brother with no harm done so they swarmed around him, all trying to
hug some part of him, and everybody was crying with joy, for they wore
their hearts upon their faces, an openness to which she was not
accustomed. But when they saw Marianne, they drew back. Jewel let
go of her hand to embrace his brother, who was about Marianne's age;
she stood still and let him go on, down to the river, and the tribe surged
with him and left her behind.

Men, women and children continued to stream from the house. A
brown, naked child, sodden from the river, bounced up into Jewel's arms
and he hugged her. She wondered if this could be his own daughter for
he kissed her with the greatest affection and laughed. The ground was
marshy and gave beneath Marianne's feet.

Some of the people glanced back at her and made vague, fluttering,
protective gestures. The sun was shining but she felt very cold. A little
boy about four years old made a sudden dart at her and ripped a strip
off her skirt before she could stop him. He retreated a few yards,
squatted down and chewed at the relic as if expecting some immediate
magic effect from it while he shot her glances of be-wilderment and
fright. But most of the tribe ignored her completely. They all began
to wade back across the river and she was left alone, for Jewel appeared

to have quite forgotten her since he was so glad to be home.

The middle-aged woman she had seen on the road came from the house. She was enveloped in a large apron of astonishing whiteness and her sleeves were rolled up, revealing forearms of great strength and size. She ran along the terrace and down the crumbling steps with the flapping, ungainly run of a fat woman; although Marianne was so far away from her, she could see the woman's grey hair uncoiling from the bun on top of her head. The people parted to let her through and she hugged Jewel harder than any of them. Then she looked across the river and Marianne saw the clean woman's forefinger pointing at her. Jewel at once turned and hurried back.

'You forgot me,' she said, accusingly.

'I was overcome,' he replied. 'It's not every day you rise from the dead. Can you still walk?'

But she found it very difficult to start walking again once she had stopped. He carried her over the river and set her down in front of the clean woman, whose name was Mrs Green. She was his foster-mother. She had a broad, doughy face covered with freckles. She kissed Marianne; she smelled of baking.

'Don't be scared,' she said. 'He's not a bad boy at heart; none of them are bad boys, in spite of appearances.'

The little girl clambered up Jewel's trunk as simply as if it were that of a tree and sat on his shoulders, pulling his hair. He slapped her. Marianne was now so dizzy the brown faces danced around her like dead leaves. When the Barbarians saw Mrs Green had not turned to stone as a result of her kiss, they clustered round Marianne with a braver curiosity and she felt moist, exploring hands on her arms, legs and bare neck and somebody tugging at the crude bandage on her leg.

'Leave her alone,' said Jewel. 'The snake bit her but she didn't die.'

He gave them this information contemptuously but they hushed and drew away from her. The crowd now began gradually to melt away, going back to former occupations such as tanning hide, sharpening knives and making pots, while Jewel, his foster-mother, his half-brother and Mrs Green's grandchild, the little girl, went towards the house.

'And Joseph,' said Jewel. 'How is Joseph?'

'Blue all over,' said Precious. 'It's no joke, I can tell you.'

'Dead by night, I reckon,' said Mrs Green. 'Oh, my poor boy. And such pain and Donally won't leave him alone nor ease him, either.'

'And him only twenty-two years old,' said Jewel. 'The first of us to go.'

Mrs Green put her hand confidentially on Jewel's arm and her voice sank to a whisper.

'Jewel, my love, ease him.'

'I won't kill him!' he said.

Marianne stumbled and cried out. They ignored her.

'You mean I should put him out of his misery like a horse with a broken leg, ease him with death, is it? With a knife, or a gun, which would be best, do you think?'

'It's a brother's duty,' said Mrs Green sententiously. 'You don't need to lose your temper, do you. I'd do it myself, but it's no job for a woman and, besides, Donally won't let me into the room.'

Jewel changed moods with extreme swiftness. He stood in the benign sunshine and, though tears of joy were still drying on his cheeks, he exuded the bleakest despair.

'I won't kill him,' he said. 'No, never.'

'Ease him, my love,' she said, as if she had not heard him. 'You know what I mean.'

The small group went on walking towards the house.

'Such pain you never saw,' said the old woman. 'And calling out longingly for death to come. It is your duty; he is your responsibility.'

Jewel put his hand over her mouth to shut her up.

'Take care of the girl, then. Give her something to eat and put her to bed or she'll be ill, too, and what's to be done, then?'

'I'm coming with you to make sure,' said Mrs Green. 'Didn't I feed Joseph my own milk when he was a baby, like I did you? Isn't he flesh of my flesh, almost? Here, our Jen, take the girl up to my room and make her lie down.'

The old woman and the two young men broke into a run without a backward glance and went up the stairs to the terrace to vanish through the grandiloquent doorway of the house, where a worm-eaten door hung open off its hinges. Marianne was left alone with the child, who plumped down on the grass beside her with a sigh. She wore nothing but a daisy chain. She had ringworm.

'You're from the Professors,' she told Marianne firmly. She had a very deep voice for so young a child.

'Yes,' said Marianne.

'You killed my father,' said Jen accusingly.

'Not I, myself,' said Marianne with a contraction of the heart she did not understand. 'They did it out of self-protection.'

'He dressed up and went away and he didn't come back and the Professors had killed him and baked him and eaten him with salt,' said Jen firmly. 'That's what my mother said.'

'That's what they all say,' said Marianne, but she did not pacify the child, whose face contorted as she spat. The gob of saliva clung to Marianne's skirt like a weird gemstone. Jen walked away with dignity. There was an open sore on her backside. Marianne was sick with pain and alone. She dragged herself up the staircase in front of the house by the rotten stone handrail. Her eyes kept misting over and she thought she saw furred animals inside the front door but she was mistaken; all that met her when she entered the house was the reek of open sewers.

The Barbarians did not wonder why the house still existed; it offered them shelter so they moved in and filled it with the smoke of their fires and their abominable refuse. The hall was very dark but Marianne could make out some old carvings on the walls and a curving marble staircase sweeping upwards. The smell of roasting meat mingled with that of ordure. She was still clutching her sprig of honeysuckle and she pressed it against her face, smelling the outdoors upon it. A woman came from the shadows at the back of the hall, raised her heavy skirt, squatted and urinated.

'Where has Jewel gone?' asked Marianne.

The woman wobbled in the middle of the spreading puddle, made the sign against the evil eye and wailed.

'Oh, don't be stupid,' said Marianne angrily. 'I'm flesh and blood and I want to find Jewel.'

The woman seemed impressed by Marianne's anger and said: 'Up-stairs, in Donally's room.' She glanced warily at the young girl before she darted back through a doorway into a black hole where there was a fire. Marianne limped upstairs and saw an open door.

Perhaps this room had been a chapel for it seemed the most ancient part of the house, a high, narrow vault of dark stone. The arched windows were covered with animal hides and the only light came from some guttering candles stuck to plane surfaces of stone. Weeds were growing out of cracks in the walls. Someone had ingeniously contrived a stove out of a large saucepan and made a funnel arrangement so that most of the smoke was taken out through a hole in the window, behind the hides; on this stove, a pot simmered and sent out a green scent of herbs which hovered on top of the reek of putrefaction which filled the room. It was as if all the appalling smells which had ever assailed her reached a peak and culmination; she had never smelled decaying flesh before. The honeysuckle dropped from her hand. A bundle of blankets lay on a mattress in the centre of the floor and she guessed this was the man who was dying of a mortifying wound.

In a corner, the young boy she had seen in the forest sat chained to a staple in the wall, gnawing upon a bone. There were rushes on the floor and everywhere a litter of books, bottles, vessels, strangely shaped utensils and bundles of dried plants. The youngest brother pushed past her abruptly, leaned over the banister of the staircase and vomited lengthily into the hall. She could make out nothing of what was going on in the room except for some moving figures by the improvised bed and the sudden flash of Mrs Green's apron; there was a good deal of confusion, some angry voices, some terrible screams and babblings and then Marianne fainted.

Mrs Green had a room to herself because she was old and dignified. She also insisted upon a proper chamberpot of her own. She kept a faded photograph of the wife of a Professor of Economics for whom she had once worked in a tarnished silver frame on the wooden box in which she kept her personal belongings, a few dresses, several aprons, her hairpins and a book which was no less precious to her because she had forgotten how to read it. This book was a copy of *Great Expectations*. She also kept the first tooth which Jewel had shed, wrapped up in a twist of paper, and also a lock of his first hair.

The walls of her room were still stuck here and there with a paper of red flock, furry to the touch, which, peeling, showed huge patches of plaster where various colours of damp and rot combined to give the appearance of a gigantic bruise. While Mrs Green bathed Marianne's leg with warm water and put clean bandages on it, she stared at this bruise, which changed its shapes continually and all were familiar but none were recognizable.

Mrs Green gave up her own bed to Marianne, a hay-stuffed mattress spread with linen sheets and some blankets, all stolen. While Marianne was ill, she stayed with her much of the time and, though she rarely spoke to her, she sometimes sang her lullabies like those her nurse had sung. Marianne was very ill for a long time and sometimes delirious, when she would confuse Mrs Green with her nurse and be either comforted or distressed according to whether she remembered her childhood or her nurse's last days. When she was delirious, the room would also fill with multiple images of snakes and knives or would become the forest and she alone in it. But one night she woke from an unusually deep and dreamless sleep and saw that the room, though full of unpredictable shadows and silence, was only a room with red walls and a fire was alight in the hearth.

The companion of her journey crouched before it. She knew him immediately. Mrs Green, a solid and at last unmistakable figure, sat beside him on a chunk of wood cut from a piece of tree and slowly combed out his long, black hair. She held his head on her aproned knees and the firelight lent them both a dramatic yet dignified chiaroscuro. Marianne raised herself on her elbow to watch them, for she had never seen anything so ancient or so romantic, except in woodcuts at the head of ballads in her father's rarest books.

'The girl's woken up,' observed Mrs Green. 'My, she's a lucky girl to get over a snakebite.'

'Is she all right?' he asked drowsily.

Marianne nodded. She was lucid and recovered; she knew herself to be well again and thinking coherently.

'She's a tough little girl,' said Jewel. 'I'll say that for her.'

'She's a long way from home,' said Mrs Green. 'And I'll thank you to keep your hands off her, my duck; you just watch out.'

'And did your brother die, in the end?' asked Marianne, and shivered.

Jewel looked down at his fingers and she realized she had been tactless.

'Oh, yes. He died before I had to exercise the dubious prerogative of mercy. All I had to do was dig his grave. I'm the public executioner, see, and also the fucking grave-digger.'

'Watch your language in front of the young lady!' exclaimed Mrs Green.

He glanced at her as if amazed and laughed, but the laughter turned into another shattering fit of coughing. He fell on the floor and was wracked, while Mrs Green clucked uselessly and Marianne, watching him writhe, choke and gasp, thought remotely: 'He's going to die young.'

3

'The thing to remember about them is, they don't think,' said Mrs Green. 'They jump from one thing to the next like kids jumping stepping stones and so they go on until they fall in the water.'

'Does Jewel never think, although he is educated?'

'Sometimes he does,' said Mrs Green. She was taking in the seams of an embroidered shirt so that Marianne would have something to wear. She used needles from a little case she had carefully kept with her since one wild night when she was eighteen years old and she saw her home burning and her husband's head shot clean from his shoulders. Since her husband had been an old man who often beat her and demanded unnatural practices in bed, she had then said: 'Take me with you' to some horseman as he reloaded his rifle and he lifted her up behind his saddle and subsequently gave her a number of children until another night attack, from which he never returned. And this was how Mrs Green first arrived in the tribe.

'Sometimes Jewel thinks but usually he gets the Doctor to do his thinking for him.'

A cold, wet wind blew in through the glassless window. Outside, it was raining; it was a cold, wet summer's day. The shirt in Mrs Green's hands was of fine wool, originally woven and sewn in a Professor village for intellectuals to wear but now it was covered all over with red and yellow daisies and little chips of mirror, a gaudy and totally changed garment.

'They like bright colours, see,' said Mrs Green with faint disparagement. 'Bright colours, beads, things that shine. They're like kids, I tell you.'

The colours of the Professors were browns and sepias, black, white and various shades of grey. All the clothes Marianne had ever worn were muted and restrained and Mrs Green still dressed herself in dark shades, as if she refused to capitulate to the tribe at some final point. Perhaps somewhere in her mind she still hoped for another change. She talked about the tribe with detachment, although she was a woman of authority within it.

'And I'd have run away if Jewel had been killed. They're little kids that believe the first thing that comes into their heads, and I don't trust the Doctor, I never have. I told Jewel to bump him off years ago but he wouldn't, not after his dad died even, not even then he wouldn't. And everyone else too scared. It'd be hell with your Dr Donally running everything, real hell, no respect for the old or nothing. Only tortures, mutilations and displays of magic.'

Marianne raised her eyebrows to hear this.

'Hell,' repeated Mrs Green. 'Hell on earth.'

Her use of the word 'hell' indicated to Marianne that Mrs Green had belonged to one of the fiery religious sects that still flowered among some Professor communities, and, more exotically, among the Barbarians, also. These sects held in common the belief that the war had been the wrath of the Lord. The communities maintained Professors of Theology while the Barbarians (it was said) practised human sacrifice. Marianne recalled descriptions of hell in her father's books, a place of fire and torment. The hard rain rattled into the room.

'Would you have run away to the Professors, back to where you came from?'

Mrs Green stopped sewing for a moment and gazed at her needle as if recollecting the first things she had sewn with it.

'You don't understand a mother's heart,' she said. Her speech was studded with commonplaces.

'No, but would you?'

'I'm too old to change back, now,' said Mrs Green. 'I've got used to the travelling and all. I'd have taken, perhaps, my granddaughter, my little Jen, and gone down to the coast. Jen's mother doesn't take good care of her, she's soft in the head, Jen's mother, and Jen's father, my son, that was, he's dead. I'd have gone to the coast, I've got a daughter that married into the fishermen down there. Perhaps that's where I'd go, if Jewel got killed, ever.'

'And do you trust none of the other brothers? Aren't they your foster-sons, too?'

'Wild boys,' said Mrs Green. 'Wild boys, all.'

Marianne sat covered with furs against the cold while Mrs Green talked in a gentle, murmurous stream, talk of an old woman starved for company, and every other word she said betrayed her passion for her eldest foster-son. Marianne unblocked the dam; she said:

'How can a man call himself Jewel without embarrassment?'

'Jewel Lee Bradley, his mother was a Lee. The Lees are Old Believers, they're clannish but they've got class. They were travellers before the war, you see. Jewel's his mother's boy, though he doesn't recall her; she was ever such a good-looking woman and that pleased to see a boy, since she'd had two girls before. Both of which died. But she was so pleased to see a boy she called him Jewel, her Jewel. And then she died herself, poor thing; she had him and never stopped bleeding. All her blood ran out of her womb and I suckled her boy, since one of my own just died. They're all dark, the Bradleys, like their father, old Bradley, he was black as pitch but then, he rarely washed, if ever. All the same, black as pitch under the dirt. And all the Lees are light on their feet and graceful, he gets that from his mother. And good with horses, the Lees are famous for it. Tamers of horses.'

Marianne was interested to find evidence of a Barbarian snobbery. If Jewel was an orphan of the hurricane, he was also one of its aristocrats, which might account for the extreme arrogance of his bearing. He did not come to get his foster-mother to comb his hair for him again; nobody visited her now she was well for now she was a prisoner. A hard scab covered the wound on her leg and she could walk as well as ever but Mrs Green still would not let her out of her room and Marianne no longer had any clear idea of how long she had been there.

If time was frozen among the Professors, here she lost the very idea of time, for the Barbarians did not segment their existence into hours nor even morning, afternoon and evening but left it raw in original shapes of light and darkness so the day was a featureless block of action and night of oblivion. Marianne was fastened into the room by means of the trunks of some trees which were placed across the door outside and she was left quite alone, for, now she was no longer sick, Mrs Green occupied herself with her other duties about the house and only came to Marianne to bring her sad, heavy food or to lie down beside her on the mattress and sleep. The weather continued bad; she watched mists of rain shift and coalesce.

As it grew dark, apparitions of horsemen appeared between the melting trees. Leaving the woods, they crossed the river, their horses loaded with carcasses of deer, wild pig and sheep; and men in their dripping furs were so plastered with mud they seemed not men at all but rather emanations of the shaggy forest. Mud and weariness rendered every one anonymous and the wide, wet brims of their felt hats hid their faces; she could never distinguish Jewel among them. Miserable dogs lolloped beside them and they rode in silence.

She felt herself removed to a different planet. Here, the very air had a different substance, dank, chill and subtly flavoured with ordure, to be choked down, like bad food, rather than breathed easily. Even the flames in the hearth formed a different kind of fire, when Mrs Green lit it, a fire which menaced as it warmed and did not warm sufficiently while it puffed out such piercingly acrid smoke her eyes were always watering. Sounds drifted into the room, raucous cries and the neighing of horses. Sometimes she heard ferocious inhuman howlings, she thought these were the cries of wolves outside in the forest. And sometimes she thought she heard music which seemed to come from within the house itself, though often she confused it with the sound of the wind sighing in the branches outside. If Jewel did not come to visit her, then neither did his tutor; it was as though she were in quarantine.

'Well, Donally reckons it's all right for you to come downstairs in the morning,' said Mrs Green one night, taking bone pins from her coil of hair which then fell down in thin, grey wisps round her creased neck. 'But, here – I'll say this, never eat anything that I haven't cooked for you myself, nor given you with my own hands. And you keep beside me, mind, don't go running off.'

'Why?'

'It's what you might call a health precaution,' said Mrs Green. She shrouded herself in a voluminous flannel nightdress and blew out the flame of the small, foul lamp. This lamp was nothing but a lint wick floating in a saucer of animal fat. Then the old woman lay down beside

Marianne; Marianne could just make out the shimmer of her fleshy back, a stout wall.

She watched Mrs Green prepare her some breakfast in the empty kitchen where the huntsmen had eaten hours before. Mrs Green used a metal pot over an open fire; she mixed flour from a sack stolen from those who had effortfully tilled the soil, kept good seed and sown it, reaped, harvested, milled, bagged and then been deprived, though they were the rightful bakers and eaters of the flour and its subsequent bread if there was such a thing as natural justice. Nevertheless, Mrs Green scooped up a handful of flour by right of conquest, since the need of the Barbarians was greater. To make her bread, she mixed the flour with salt, water and animal fat in a bowl of very rough pottery.

'Bread's a bit of a luxury,' she said, but her unleavened bread was only a sour kind of biscuit. She also made a thin porridge with some other grain; this porridge tasted principally of smoke. There was cold meat. There was some milk for Marianne, though it was poor milk and Mrs Green mixed it with water to make it go further. Marianne sat at an immense, foundering table and ate the strange food that was now her regular diet.

The kitchen was more a cave. There was still glass in most of the windows but this glass was now so caked with the grime of years that only the great fire crackling on the hearth and the door, open to the morning, gave any light. Joints of meat either undergoing the process of smoking or smoked already hung everywhere from hooks and huge, lacquered bluebottles buzzed about. A few pieces of worm-eaten furniture still remained and the ancient dresser was still mysteriously loaded with cracked and ancient pottery which the tribe was too super-stitious to utilize. There was a large sink full of a brilliant moss which also coated the flagstones underfoot with emeraldine fur. There was a smell of earth, of rotting food and of all-pervading excrement. Marianne drew herself coldly inside her skin and ate because to do so was necessary though by no means pleasant.

The child Jen sat on the table and squinted inquisitively at her. It was another cold day and Jen wore a tunic of long-haired fur that made her look like a little Ancient Briton. Marianne contemplated the archaic child and wondered if her clothing were proof of the speed with which the Barbarians were sinking backwards or evidence of their adaption to new conditions. Then Jen slapped her hand. She spilled a spoonful of porridge.

'I don't like it when you stare at me,' said Jen.

'I don't like it when you stare at me, either,' snapped Marianne, furious.

'Here, do I have to be friends with her?' Jen asked her grandmother plaintively. Mrs Green watched a pan of bread cooking over the fire; the flames threw her shadow across the wall.

'I dunno,' said Mrs Green. 'I'm not sure, nobody's told me.'

'What, the old man didn't say?'

'Nobody's told me nothing except she's to be looked after,' said Mrs Green with a sigh. She stared at the girl and the child thoughtfully, considering; suddenly she issued a brusque and arbitrary order.

'Give her a kiss. Go on. She's real.'

Melodramatic amounts of smoke billowed from the chimney, blackening the bread with soot. Jen gave an astonished caw and flinched. The flinch persisted until it became a shudder; shuddering, she drew back, crawling backwards across the table, out of both daylight and firelight off into the shadow. She drew back so far she slipped off the far edge of the table, turned tail and fled from the kitchen into the passage. Her bare feet thudded softly on the stone as they receded into the depths of the house. Mrs Green shrugged, emptied the contents of the pan of bread on to a wooden dish and began to scrape off the soot with a knife.

'Anyone can make mistakes,' she said. 'Thought she might give you a kiss, see. Thought it might make you seem more natural.'

Marianne perceived the child defined her as a witch, a definition which was in error but still reasonable from the child's point of view. She felt a certain derisive pleasure. A dog came and nosed at her knee; she gave it the remains of her breakfast and the meal was over. Then the dog lifted its leg to urinate against the leg of the table and Mrs Green threw a dipperful of water at it, besides a volley of abuse.

She decided Mrs Green's position was that of a housekeeper or, perhaps, more properly, some kind of domestic matriarch. All day long, Mrs Green walked about the house inspecting things; the house was a camp on several different levels. Under the broken, moulded ceilings, the camp-fires of the ephemeral caravanserai flickered and reared and all appeared transitory though, if home was where the heart was, the children seemed sufficiently loved. The households were at work. Women prepared furs by various primitive methods, scraping away the flesh from the pelts with small knives. Others embroidered cloth with designs of cocks, roses, suns, cakes, knives, snakes and acorns. This seemed frivolous work to Marianne but it was carried out with as much concentration as that of curing the pelts; later, she found these designs had magic significance, though she probably would scarcely have believed this had she been told it the first day. Some old men were engaged in carving cups and platters from wood. Others had their hands up to the elbows in clay, for pottery. All the activity in the house was conducted in silence for there was little need to talk and very little to talk about, anyway. The adult men either worked outside with the horses or had gone to the woods, hunting.

The small family groups lived in such close contact the children were held almost in common. If one fell down and bruised itself and started to cry, the first woman to hand would take it into her arms and comfort it. But two of the babies were very sick. They lay in withy baskets and weakly puked their milk. Mrs Green gazed at them with fear and sadness, while the mother of one of the babies kept one hand defensively on a talisman hanging round her neck and trembled to see Marianne. This woman was perhaps a year or so younger than she, certainly very young. She had snakes tattooed around her wrists; the tail of each snake disappeared succinctly into its own mouth. She wore no stockings or shoes. Her dress was made of a stolen blanket patterned with large dark blue and black checks, a dress as rectangular in design as a box, cut deep at the breast for nursing. Her right knee showed through a tear. She wore a dead wrist watch on her arm, purely for decoration; it was a little corpse of time, having stopped for good and all at ten to three one distant and forgotten day. She had only one eye, the other was covered by a black patch. Marianne could hardly believe she and this woman were both of the same sex. She was heavily pregnant again, though her sick baby was less than a year old. Marianne guessed the baby was suffering from some gastric disorder.

'I should keep them warm, if I were you,' said Mrs Green.

The woman moved first one basket, then the other, to the side of a glum fire in a ruined fireplace which filled the room with a sour fog of smoke. There was no glass at all in these windows, only some rusting iron bars across them. Ghosts of clowns and rabbits in top hats were fading from the torn wallpaper; the room must have been a nursery at some former time. There were straw pallets, a metal pot and various items of clothing scattered over the floor.

'Empty that!' said Mrs Green sharply, pointing to a pail of excrement. She spoke too sharply; the woman muttered mutinously under her breath as she took the plashing pail outside on to the landing and pitched the contents over into the well of the hall. When she returned, she took two charms from the dozen or so upon her person and slipped them beneath the babies' blankets.

'The Doctor's coming in later to say a prayer,' she said. 'But better to be safe than sorry.'

Mrs Green's dress came down to her ankles. She held it up as she walked through the corridors since there was so much filth underfoot, ashes, pieces of fur, offal of beasts and so on. But the women made some sporadic attempts to keep the actual living quarters clean, though Marianne's skin itched at the thought of vermin. The thin mattresses, stuffed with leaves, hay, straw or wool, must engender gigantic colonies of bugs; the flowing Barbarian coiffures, clogged at the roots with lice, now seemed wilfully perverse accessories and when she saw warrior garments hanging limply from nails hammered into the walls, she almost laughed to see the fragile shells of such poorly founded terror. The children suffered promiscuously from ringworm, skin diseases and weeping eye. Also rickets. She considered the possibility of deficiency diseases such as pellagra and beri-beri. When she thought of the noble savage in her father's researches, her distaste was mixed with grief.

'It's all very different from what you've been accustomed to, dear,' said Mrs Green, ducking beneath a washing-line in a corridor on which hung pieces of leather cured by a process utilizing dung of dog.

'Yes,' replied Marianne through pinched lips.

'But then, you should see the way the Out People live, if living you call it. Huddled in holes in the ground, nursing their sores. They poison their arrows by dipping the heads in their sores, it's well known.'

They visited every room in the fetid warren except the one where the Doctor lived, though, passing across his landing, Marianne was surprised to see a sign in red paint, written on the wall. This sign said: BOREDOM IS THE HANDSOME SON OF PRIDE. Since the Barbarians were illiterate, she supposed Donally must have scrawled it up exclusively for her own benefit. She very much wanted to visit Dr Donally but Mrs Green did not even suggest it. As the house filled with darkness, the hunters came home with the day's meat.

They brought their catch into the kitchen. They slung carcass after carcass on to the table, where the stiff limbs stuck up straight into the air and the eyes glazed in the final stare of fear. The fire was lavishly stoked to give more light as the beasts were apportioned among the close kin groups and then skinning and butchering began. The brothers took the roles of sharers and dividers and the whole tribe seemed suddenly gathered in the room, quarrelling over the joints, demanding and protesting while the brothers roughly chopped the flesh with axes that first caught the firelight and flashed but soon grew dim and ruddy. The kitchen was transformed into an abattoir. Bones still curded with meat, antlers, tusks of pigs and rags of bloody pelts were cast to the ground in charnel heaps and the small children shrieked and danced around them in a frenzy of excitement.

The six brothers, all black as their common father, now grew red with the blood that dewed everything. All the eyes in every face around her reflected nothing and the faces themselves, deformed or leaden, blanched or ablaze, were riven by vile, twisted mouths from which issued harsh screeches or foul abuse, faces stained with blood or fire and then blotted out by shadow. Marianne's bewildered senses reported only a whirling conflict of black and red. Then her senses themselves became so confused she seemed to smell the hot stench of red itself and hear the incomprehensible sound of black in the raised, tumultuous voices around her. Jewel, Johnny, Jacob, Bendigo, Blue and Precious. The weird litany of the brothers' names repeated itself over and over again in her head. She did not know the name of the dead one and they seemed to have forgotten him already. They flung parcels of offal to the dogs. A dog raced away with a crimson set of lungs between its teeth, to consume them in the privacy of the privy. Marianne tried to creep towards the open back door to escape into the silence and freshness of the night but Mrs Green saw her and trapped her firmly by the wrist and she had to wait until all was over, the food shared out, the crowd dispersed, the brothers sluicing themselves with water from the barrel and shaking themselves dry.

Mrs Green perched Marianne on a chair and left her there while she swilled down the floor. The brothers, half-naked, approached the fire, to warm themselves. They had the rolling walk of men more accustomed to horseback than solid ground. Two had abstract marks of blue tattooing on their cheeks, all had tattooing on their bodies, patterns of snakes, birds, suns and stars. One had a moustache and three others full beards. She could only count five and realized Jewel had vanished. She felt poorly protected.

The brothers eyed her circumspectly and she saw the youngest, Precious, furtively make the sign against the evil eye. Precious was brown, young and tender and she was sorry he was the most superstitious for he had pulled one of the malformed roses from the garden and stuck it behind his ear. They grouped about the fire, saying nothing. Trickles of bloody water ran down the room to Marianne's feet; she tucked her feet beneath her as she balanced on the chair, one leg of which was broken.

Then that terrible howling she had heard before rose up outside, near at hand, an intense and anguished wail which swelled to an intolerable climax and died away again, foundering in hoarse sobs. Bendigo, or perhaps it was Blue, spat into the fire.

'I wish Donally would come down and see to the kid,' he said.

'Is that a child crying?' exclaimed Marianne, shocked into speech.

'It's the half-wit,' said Precious indifferently. 'It's his kid, isn't it. It's the Doctor's half-wit.'

'The half-wit's outside, see,' said Mrs Green, now scouring the table with handfuls of grass. 'He's feeling it tonight, poor thing, the weather and all.'

The arc of wordless sound rose up once more, like a vile rainbow. Marianne sprang from the chair, darted past the congregation of brothers and looked out of the kitchen door.

Outside, it was still light enough to see a paved courtyard full of weeds, surrounded by tumble-down out-buildings. When she had seen the boy of the forest chained to the wall in Donally's room, she had thought he was a hallucination; now she saw him again, squatting on the paving stones at the end of his chain, which was fastened to a staple in the side of a shed. The boy rolled his eyes until they were all whites and howled at the darkening sky. Gnawed bones lay all round him. There was a dish of water before him and another, empty, marked 'Dog', in which he must receive his food. Rain splashed on his shoulders and down his thin chest, which showed a greenish pallor between the tattooings. He squatted, howled and then fell silent, picking at dirt between his toes. He was quite real.

'He fouled his bedding, see,' explained another brother mysteriously materialized beside her, watching so she did not go outside. 'He fouled his bedding, he can't live in with the Doctor, can he, not if he fouls his bedding. The Doctor is nothing if not fastidious.'

'He's got a constitution of iron, the half-wit,' remarked another brother. On her other side, a brother so covered with hair she could only see his eyes. She glanced around; she was surrounded. She moved away from the door and they walked with her, so close she could smell them. They smelled of the grave. Mrs Green looked up anxiously from her cleaning. A bough fell in the fire; sparks spurted up.

The atmosphere in the devilish kitchen splintered and jagged. She tried to duck beneath a man's arm to run to Mrs Green but he caught hold of her shoulders and Mrs Green did nothing except make a despairing gesture, although she had warned Jewel off Marianne before. Wild boys. Eyes like dead wood and grinning mouths equipped with the whitest teeth, everywhere Marianne looked she saw eyes like dead wood fixed on her face and cruel mouths. She glanced towards the inner door to ascertain perhaps another means of escape and there she saw the sixth, or the seventh, counting the one who was dead. He had entered silently and now leaned against the wall, almost hidden, watching also, cleaning his nails with the point of a knife and watching her.

'Johnny . . .' said Mrs Green in a sad, coaxing voice. 'Jacob . . .'

Precious made the sign against the evil eye, again, but that was all. They stirred and rustled. They had laid aside their rifles but all were armed with knives and they appeared to hate her.

'There are sick children in the house,' offered Mrs Green pathetically, as though this was sufficient reason to dissuade them from rape and possibly murder. Marianne saw Jewel throw back his head and laugh with apparently pure pleasure at the tone of this remark. As if his laughter were a signal, the three beside the fire began to move towards her and the man on her left, Johnny, or perhaps it was Jacob, deliberately put his hand beneath the opening of her embroidered shirt and felt her right breast. Firelight shadow monsters galloped along the walls. All gasped and came closer.

They directed her inexorably towards the table. Mrs Green wrung her hands and emitted small mews of distress but she, too, was ambivalent; she would be distressed but also perhaps obscurely satisfied at what would certainly take place. Marianne discovered she was not in the least frightened, only very angry indeed, and began to struggle and shout; at this the brothers laughed but did not cease to crowd in on her. So she closed her eyes and pretended she did not exist.

But this desperate device for self-protection proved unnecessary. Suddenly all laughter ceased and, silent, the men fell away from her. Mrs Green burst into screeches of relief and Marianne smelled a curiously sweet odour of lavender. She opened her eyes and saw the giant with the parti-coloured beard sitting on the edge of the table as if it were a throne, carrying one of the little lamps in his hand. The oil in this lamp smelled of lavender. The brothers had retreated to a corner in a cowed group.

'They're brave, grant them that,' said the giant. 'It's a well-known fact that Professor women sprout sharp teeth in their private parts, to bite off the genitalia of young men.'

Jewel laughed once again, though nobody else did. He entered the circle of the Doctor's light. His hair was now fastened into two stiff plaits and he looked very much like pictures of American Indians which Marianne had seen in her father's books. In this context, his name was no more surprising than would have been Handsome Lake, Rain in the Face or He Who Puts Out and Kills. Like such Indians, his face revealed no emotion. Donally aimed a playful punch at his ribs.

'And you, what would you have done had they fallen to it? Alleviated your boredom by applauding the spectacle?'

His voice was perfectly cultured, thin, high and soft. Presumably to preserve his secrecy, he wore a pair of dark glasses with wire frames, one lens of which was cracked clean across. He had a thin, mean and cultured face. Marianne had grown up among such voices and faces. She said the first thing that came into her head.

'Why don't you take more care of your child?'

'Because he has disgusting habits,' replied the Doctor crisply. 'He bites the hand that feeds and wallows in his own mire.'

She might have been at home, in her tower, discussing with visitors a dog that refused to be house-trained, except that speech revealed Donally filed his teeth to points. He extended his hand to her; it was a soft, white hand and the fingernails were carefully trimmed and manicured. After a moment, she extended her own hand and he shook it formally. He reached into an inner pocket beneath his handsome coat of gleaming black fur, took out a pigskin wallet and, from this, a card, which he offered her. It was a white visiting card on which was beauti-fully engraved, in Gothic script, DR F. R. DONALLY, PH D. After she read it, he took it back.

'Marianne,' he said warmly. He gestured round the room and com-pany, smiling. 'However, you must feel more like Miranda.'

'You must have been a Professor of Literature, once,' she said.

'Well, here I am and here I stay,' he replied pleasantly.

He seemed in a jovial mood and kept playfully touching the beautiful young man who stood beside him, now and then stroking his shoulders and head, attentions Jewel ignored. Marianne was almost relieved to encounter once again the kind of man with whom she was most familiar, and he seemed perfectly at home, sitting on the table waiting for his supper, even though they defined him as a shaman, or else he had decided so to define himself. She began to bite her fingernails; he clicked his tongue against his teeth.

'Come, now, can't have you with bitten fingernails, when you're our little holy image, dear.'

'What's that?'

'You heard him,' said Jewel.

'Our lady of the wilderness,' amplified Donally with a delighted smile. 'The virgin of the swamp.'

'Just as well they didn't rape me, then,' she snapped.

'Quite so,' said Donally. 'Familiarity breeds contempt. You'll have to remain terrifying, you know; otherwise, what hope is there for you?'

Mrs Green was now preparing the evening meal, arranging a joint of pork to roast over the fire, and the other brothers, still silent and casting intermittent and malign regards towards the girl and her companions, settled down on the floor with a lamp in the middle of the circle. They began to play some game of chance with pieces of bones and argued in soft voices about the throws. The smell of roasting meat mingled with the other smells. A dog or two wandered around. Jewel kicked away one who sniffed at him. At the slightest movement, the trinkets with which he was covered made a small, jingling sound, so Marianne realized with her ears more than her eyes how still he ordinarily remained.

'Fear,' remarked Jewel suddenly, as if proposing a topic for discussion.

'The ruling passion,' responded Donally courteously. 'I can provoke an ecstasy of dread by raising my little finger but then, I've worked hard and bided my time.'

The pork fat crackled deliciously. Donally raised and let fall one of Jewel's heavy black plaits.

'Go on, tell her about religion being a social necessity,' said Jewel.

'Not yet,' said Donally. 'She looks tired.'

'Had a bad day?' inquired Jewel with some irony.

'I haven't decided, yet.'

'That's a clever answer,' applauded Donally.

'I told you she was clever.'

'You're a gift from the unknown, young lady,' said Dr Donally, smiling sufficiently to reveal his curiously uncompromising teeth. 'You provide these unfortunate people with a focus for the fear and resentment they feel against their arbitrary destiny.'

He coughed, as in a lecture theatre.

'Here, Donally,' said Jewel. 'They killed her father, back where she lived. They cut him up with an axe.'

He turned his head towards his tutor with a faint chink of jewellery and still no expression on his face; Donally put out his long, white, tender hand again and stroked Jewel's cheek.

'What are you thinking of, now?'

'Regicide,' the other answered.

'Don't let's exaggerate,' chided Donally mildly. To Marianne, he said: 'Look at him, he's the Duke of Little Egypt, he's the king of a rainy country, he's inherited the earth.'

He went off into peals of mirth and, reluctantly, Jewel laughed also. Both their faces grew so twisted and ugly with incomprehensible laughter that Marianne, disquieted, decided then and there she had no reason or desire to stay any longer in this disgusting and dangerous place.

Next morning, she found that one of the sick babies was roasting with a terrific fever while the other was limp and white. Three other babies were showing the same initial symptoms of vomiting and looseness of the bowels.

'It's the bad water,' said Mrs Green authoritatively. 'You should get water from the spring, not from the river.'

'The Doctor says –' said the pregnant woman. She did not tell them what Donally said but when she looked at Marianne she quivered with fear. Marianne supposed the woman believed she had brought the sickness with her.

'It's time to go,' thought Marianne. 'Now. Immediately!'

For however dangerous the open country might be, she would be safer there than among these strangers; whatever romantic attraction the idea of the Barbarians might have held for her as she sat by herself in the white tower, when her father was alive, had entirely evaporated. She was full of pity for them but, more than anything, she wanted to escape, as if somewhere there was still the idea of a home. So she ran away into the wood, not much caring if the wild beasts ate her; but Jewel found her, raped her and brought her back with him.

Yet she had taken a great deal of care to go secretly. She took her clothes, some blankets and some food. Mrs Green was far too busy with the sick babies to keep guard over her and, when she asked if she could go and rest by herself the next afternoon, the old woman nodded abstractedly and Marianne slipped unnoticed from the house by the back door.

It was a bright day of sunshine and soft air. The golden weeds in the courtyard scattered pollen on the green skin of the boy on the chain, who lay asleep on the sun-warmed stones, his hair floating out in a muddy puddle. There were marks of a recent beating on his body. If she had had a knife, she would have tried to set him free but she had no knife. It was the middle of the day and nobody saw her go; the children were down by the river and the women, also, for they took advantage of the change in the weather to do their washing, cleaning the clothes by beating them against stones in the running water. She went up into the woods at the back of the house; she climbed the hillside and looked behind her. She saw the crumbling mansion, the dung heap, some horses grazing and the busy river but the whole valley wore to her the aspect of a vast midden. She hurried to put the crest of the hill between herself and the Barbarians.

The farther she went, the happier she grew. The beautiful sun glowed through the leaves which were just beginning, here and there, to turn to gold. A great part of the summer had passed outside time and known space, in illness, isolation and foul air, but now she was by herself in the sweet, curling grass, and the forest shone with berries. Fungus like apricots or splashes of crimson paint or solid frills of grey decorated trunks of trees and fallen boughs. Yellow gorse grew everywhere. If this was where the wild beasts were, it was so beautiful she could not believe they would hurt her. She tried to remember the whereabouts of the road on which she first saw the travellers but she had a poor sense of direction and would have to wander till she found it by chance, watching to spy a thinning among the trees to show her it was near.

There were no paths except those the rabbits made and the undergrowth set traps of briars, nettles and evil plants. When she wanted to rest, she climbed into a beech tree because she would be better hidden above the ground, in case the Barbarians came by. The beech tree already had leaves of solid brass. It stood at the edge of a small, open space. Secure upon a sturdy limb, she closed her eyes.

She wished she could tell her father about the true nature of the Barbarians and discuss with him the sociology of the tribe. And its psychology, also, especially that of the ragged king of nowhere and his adviser who perversely reminded her of her father, though it was only a question of tone of voice; but her father was dead. When she opened her eyes to let the tears out, she saw Jewel standing inexorably beneath a tree, as though she had dreamed him into being by thinking of him.

He leaned against the trunk of an oak on the other side of the clearing, chewing upon a stem of grass and paring his nails with a knife.

He had a rag tied round his head to keep hair and sweat out of his eyes. He had propped his long rifle against the trunk beside him, prepared for a long siege, if necessary. They regarded one another for some time.

'You've followed me from the camp,' she said at last.

'Oh, no,' he said. 'I saw you only a little way back. You've come quite a long way. I was surprised. And in a straight line, at that.'

She looked nervously round for his brothers but he came by himself. There was nowhere to go away from him, she could climb no farther up the tree. So she stayed where she was, too angry to speak.

'Isn't it a nice day?' said Jewel at last. 'After all the rain we've been having.'

He said these words as if he had learned them from a phrase book and grinned, a grimace of the face akin to a snarl. She continued to say nothing. She tore off some beech mast and pulled it to pieces.

'Of course,' he added unexpectedly, 'it smells worse indoors on a nice day.'

Marianne gave up her silence in order to abuse him.

'Nourished in the sty,' she said unpleasantly, 'I'd never have thought you'd make such fine distinctions.'

He gave her another white, unfriendly grin while he digested what she had said.

'I wasn't nourished in no sty,' he countered eventually. 'I used to sleep with the horses because I liked their faces better.'

He continued to pare his nails.

'Furthermore,' he added, 'horses are herbivorous.'

He used words with the touching pedantry of the ill-educated; high on her branch, she felt immensely superior. She glowered.

'Are you coming down?' he asked her with detached interest.

'Not until you go away.'

'What, making another bid for freedom?'

'That's right.'

'Where will you escape, though? Where will you go in this unknown desert, only wild beasts live here but for Out People, wilder than beasts. And you've got nothing to protect yourself with and no food, either.'

'I am safer here than in your house. I shall find the road, the road leads somewhere. To a village.'

'What, one of yours? Back to your own people, then?'

'Another village, not the one I left.'

'They are all much of a muchness, you know.'

'How do you know?'

'I've been to very many.'

'Only as a visitor,' she said. 'You'd always have been just passing through.'

He shrugged and put away his knife.

'Come off your bough and teach me your vocabulary,' he invited. 'Sooner or later, we might be able to converse.'

'We wouldn't have much in common,' she pointed out.

His shadow sprang out as he approached the tree, accompanied by the faintest jingling of charms and amulets. He was inevitable, like the weather, and even more ambivalent for his face was not constructed to support a smile and she could not tell what he was thinking or if he were thinking at all, even.

'We'd have to establish common ground in order to communicate as equals, of course,' he said. She heard his tutor's high, thin voice behind his uncouth one and found, to her fury, she was crying again. She exploded with tears and rage and flung herself off the tree on top of him. She took him by surprise; they fell down together in the undergrowth and struggled for a while. He gasped and coughed horribly but he was a good deal stronger than her and soon she knew she would have to return to the camp with him by force. But this did not make her any the less angry to find herself trapped beneath him with her arms pinned down to the ground behind her head.

'I think I'm the only rational woman left in the whole world,' she said, spitting the words into his face; she could have said nothing to offend him more. They had fallen beneath the surface of the long grass. He pressed her down into the rich, moist earth itself and began to unfasten her clothes.

'You're nothing but a murderer,' she said, determined to maintain her superior status at all costs.

'You'll find me the gentlest of assassins,' he replied with too much irony for she did not find him gentle at all.

Feeling between her legs to ascertain the entrance, he thrust his fingers into the wet hole so roughly she knew what the pain would be like; it was scalding, she felt split to the core but she did not make a single sound for her only strength was her impassivity and she never closed her cold eyes, although the green sun made out the substance of his face to be polished metal and she recalled the murder she had witnessed, how the savage boy stuck his knife into her brother's throat and the blood gushed out. Because she was difficult to penetrate, he spilled several hot mouthfuls of obscenities over her. Taken by force, the last shreds of interior flesh gave; he intended a violation and effected one; a tower collapsed upon her. Afterwards, there was a good deal of blood. He stared at it with something like wonder and dipped his fingers in it. She stared at him relentlessly; if he had kissed her, she would have bitten out his tongue. However, he recovered his abominable self-possession almost immediately. She began to struggle again but he held her down with one hand, half pulled off his filthy leather jacket and ripped off the sleeve of his shirt, as he had done before when he had treated her snakebite. This repetition of action would have been comic had she been in the mood to appreciate it. He held the rag between her thighs to sop up the bleeding, a bizarre piece of courtesy.

'It's a necessary wound,' he assured her. 'It won't last long.'

'It was the very worst thing that happened to me since I came away with you,' she said. 'It hurt far worse than the snakebite, because it was intentional. Why did you do it to me?'

He appeared to consider this question seriously.

'There's the matter of our traditional hatred. And, besides, I'm very frightened of you.'

'I have the advantage of you there,' said Marianne, pushing him away and endeavouring to cover herself.

'Don't be too sure,' he replied. 'I've got to marry you, haven't I? That's why I've got to take you back.'

When he saw the expression of horror which crossed her face, he laughed until silenced by a brief spasm of coughing.

'What's that?' she exclaimed.

'Donally says,' he told her when he could speak. 'Swallow you up and incorporate you, see. Dr Donally says. Social psychology. I've nailed you on necessity, you poor bitch.'

When he left her to collect his rifle, she was too weak to attempt to run away. He also picked up her bundles, which had fallen from the tree with her, and offered her his hand. She ignored it and scrambled upright. She put him at a distance with an impersonal question.

'You must use a good deal of ammunition, since you operate a hunting economy. And do you steal it all?'

'Every bullet, yes.'

'What will you do if they stop casting bullets?'

'Bows and arrows, like the Out People,' he said with disinterest for the Professors continued to cast bullets and he was prepared to cross the bridge of their ceasing to do so when he arrived at it. He mimed the gesture of drawing a long bow and watched a non-existent arrow fly off into the air. And his elegance and style in doing this were so remarkable and so archaic that, although Marianne disliked him intensely, she could not help but marvel.

'You'd take to bows and arrows like a duck to water,' she said. 'You are a complete anachronism.'

Though, as soon as she had said it, she wondered if it were true, for he blended into the landscape around them while she herself did not.

'What's an anachronism,' he said darkly. 'Teach me what an anachronism is.'

'A pun in time,' she replied cunningly, so that he would not understand her.

'Come off it,' he growled; he was by no means an intellectual.

'A thing that once had a place and a function but now has neither any more.'

'Well, well,' said Jewel, once more self-possessed. At that, they began to walk through the wood the way she had come. All the time, he repeated the word 'anachronism' over and over under his breath, as though learning it by heart, until she suspected mockery. He stopped to shoot a rabbit.

'Look, do I really have to marry you?' she asked despairingly. He dangled the dead rabbit by its hind legs; its iridescent ears trailed in the grass and blood dripped from its nose.

'So it would seem,' he replied.

She kicked a tuft of briars.

'My father said it would be a deep spiritual experience,' she remarked bitterly.

'What?'

'Defloration. And presumably marriage, for he saw the two as complementary.'

'He went in for that kind of thing, did he?' said Jewel.

'He was only married the once.'

'What I meant was, he had the time to think about things, did he?' explained Jewel laboriously.

'Thinking was his function.'

'Are they going to pickle his brain and keep it in a jar?' demanded Jewel. 'Or was he a preserved brain at the best of times?'

'Talk like that about my father and I'll kill you.'

'You wouldn't know how,' he said.

He saw another rabbit and shot it; that made two. When they came in sight of the house again, her courage almost failed her and she tried to run away. He tripped her up easily. Her face was naked with misery and nausea; he shrugged, set the muzzle of the rifle between her shoulders and walked her in this fashion into the courtyard at the back of the house. Here, Mrs Green squatted on the ground scraping food from a frying pan into the half-witted boy's dish. He raced round at the end of his chain, yelping.

'Right or wrong, he's going to get a square meal, whatever Donally says,' she said. Then, blinking, she recognized the figures before her.

'What have you been doing to her?'

Jewel lowered his rifle and laid the dead rabbits in his foster-mother's arms. Marianne stared at the ground, her face stiff with silence; he took hold of her chin, and, raising her face, forced her to look him in the eyes.

'The lady has lost her smile in the woods,' he said.

'And not only her smile, you villain,' said Mrs Green, hitting him a great blow with the back of the hand that did not hold the frying pan and rabbits. 'Haven't you got no respect for anything?'

The boy fell on his food with grunts of pleasure, elbowing away a ravenous mastiff attracted by the smell of meat. Jewel rubbed the mark on his face where his foster-mother hit him.

'It's not true, what they say about such girls,' he remarked.

'I hate you,' said Marianne.

'Very likely,' he said. 'That's only natural.'

He knelt down beside the Doctor's son and slipped his hand under the collar. The boy shook himself but went on eating. Jewel stroked and clapped the boy with his free hand and they murmured to one another at the back of their throats as if in brutish communication.

'The collar's rubbed his flesh all raw,' said Jewel. 'No wonder he howls.'

'You come inside and have a wash, dear,' said Mrs Green to Marianne. 'After all, it's not as bad as all that, is it? He's going to marry you tomorrow.'

Distressed as she was, Marianne could understand why Jewel began again to laugh. She gave him a backward glance as Mrs Green led her into the house but he did not look up. He had stopped laughing, had taken out a knife and seemed to be cutting open the collar the boy wore, unless he were slitting his throat. Marianne was in too much confusion to be quite sure which eventuality was most likely.

'That kid pulled through,' said Mrs Green. 'Isn't it a wonder. His fever just went, just went away like that and he's in a lovely, natural sleep. And the others are brighter, as well. Oh, what a blessing. Usually something like that goes through all the little ones, goes right through them all and most die.'

'Nobody will blame me for it, then, if the child has got better,' said Marianne.

'So you see how their minds work, do you, dear? They always look round for something to blame when things go badly, that's them, like kids. Like little kids. I feel so sorry for them, dear, so terribly sorry.'

They made their way gingerly through the heaped ordure in the hall and climbed up to her room. Written on the wall by Donally's door was a new slogan: ONENESS WITH DESTINY GIVES STYLE AND DISTINCTION. This time in black. Marianne did not understand it but she spat at it as she passed by.

4

As its inflictor predicted, her pain went away quite soon but her vindictiveness increased for she was more cruelly wounded in her pride than in her body and, besides, she felt herself quite trapped and entirely without hope. She remained in an agony of despair, cocooned in blankets upon the mattress in Mrs Green's room, refusing food and speech. The sunlight faded from the discoloured wall. At last Mrs Green arrived with the lamp and undressed for bed. The wick dipped and flickered; Mrs Green appeared to flicker.

'Last time you'll be sleeping with me,' said Mrs Green, intermittently visible as she was. 'Tomorrow you'll have to sleep with Jewel, won't you. That's the way of the world.'

At that, Marianne sprang up, her cold eyes sparking.

'All this is a bad dream,' she said. 'It can't happen, it didn't happen and it won't happen.'

'Young men will always take advantage, dear,' said Mrs Green. 'And we all have to take what we can get.'

She sighed. But all the same, she was as smug and comfortable as if wolves and tigers did not roam forests where no trees had grown previously and Marianne must learn to reconcile herself to everything from rape to mortality, just as her father had also told her she would have to do. Mrs Green's photograph flashed in the lamplight, picture of a woman who could have been Marianne's mother; Mrs Green might also feel a certain pleasure that her wild foster-son should marry so far above his class, pleasure and revenge, perhaps. Clearly she thought Marianne had learned a lesson and would not try to run away again for, after she had fed the girl the next morning, she left her to her own devices while she went off on her tour of inspection of the camp

Certainly Marianne did not intend to run away again yet, even though today was her wedding day, for she knew she would be tracked by cunning huntsmen, subjected, perhaps, to fresh humiliations and returned to the stinking castle once more at gun point. Instead, she went straight to the Doctor's study.

As she went down the staircase, she heard again the sound of the curious music which had haunted her during the days of her imprisonment; chords and crescendos of a small organ emanated from the chapel where Donally lived and he played with such violence the rotten stone appeared to shiver. She had never heard organ music before but she could tell the instrument was out of tune. The fugue approached its peak. Last night's sign was wiped off the wall; in its place was painted, MISTRUST APPEARANCES, THEY NEVER CONCEAL ANYTHING. She flung open the door and cried 'Charlatan!' at the top of her voice.

Her voice rang in accord with the music round the vaulted ceiling and both died away together. The room was almost in darkness, the windows quite covered with hides although outside the sun streamed down for it was another beautiful day. But here the baleful obscurity of the glow from the little stove concealed the whereabouts of the unseen organist until she saw the last patches of gilding left on a set of organ pipes gave off a faint gleam; a lighted candle was stuck by its own grease to the manual of a small, baroque organ perhaps late seventeenth or early eighteenth century in origin. She could make out the battered faces of one or two cherubim still smiling down on the worm-eaten oak. Donally prised away the candle and, holding it aloft, stepped down from the bench. His wiry hair stuck out all round his head like an immense halo of spikes. He had left off his dark glasses and seemed friendly and cheerful, which immediately made her suspicious. His son appeared, cowering, out of the shadows; he was panting and must have been working the organ pump.

'Run along and play,' said the Doctor benignly to the boy, who shot him a scared glance and bolted from the room, slamming the door behind him. He wore no collar today, though the ring of raw flesh round his neck was still fresh and he looked extremely cowed. He had one black eye.

'Maybe you were a Professor of Music, once,' said Marianne, glancing at the organ and, in spite of herself, impressed, for she had before heard only the martial sounds of her uncle's military band.

He made no reply but placed his candle on a book-littered, quaking table some distance from the altar and gestured Marianne to sit down upon his chair. She refused. In his own room, he chose to wear a neat, dark suit, a white shirt and a black tie, no talismans or jewellery at all, no fur or feathers. He lit a few more candles, enough for her to see a little by, to see the mossy pillars which held up the vaulted roof all clogged with cobwebs, the filthy rag of a flag upon a gilded pole propped against the altar, the brass eagles of a lectern turned bright green with verdigris, some shapes of figures of wax and stone in embrasures. But the small, pale candle flame served mainly to delineate the areas of artificial shadow, though Marianne could clearly inspect Donally's eyes. These were grey veined with green, like certain kinds of stones, and his eyeballs were lightly veined with red lines. She noticed he had plucked his eyebrows into neat, thin arcs, a queer vanity for a man who lived nowhere.

'Tell me why it's necessary for you to marry me to that Yahoo who raped me yesterday afternoon about what used to be teatime.'

'Consider and make the best of things,' said Donally, stroking the purple half of his beard. 'He is probably the most beautiful man left in the world.'

'You told me yourself to mistrust appearances; and his beauty didn't make it hurt less nor make it any less humiliating. The reverse, in fact.'

'Domiciled as you are among the Yahoos, you might as well be Queen of the midden. Don't you know the meaning of the word "ambition"?'

She shook her head impatiently.

'Come, come, now,' said Donally encouragingly. 'There must be something you want. Power? I can offer you a little power.'

He suggested the idea as if it were a delicious goody.

'All I want is for my father to be alive,' she said, overcome with misery; she sank down upon Donally's chair.

'Gather yourself together, young lady. Marry the Prince of Darkness. You'll find him very sophisticated. Though his sophistication has always been superior to his opportunities, he does the very best he can.'

She looked over his books and saw names she remembered from the spines in her father's study, Teilhard de Chardin, Lévi-Strauss, Weber, Durkheim and so on, all marked by fire and flood. He had been reading some books about society.

'Where do you come from, why are you here? Why didn't you stay where you belonged, editing texts or doing research? I suppose you might have been a Professor of Sociology, once, though only a crazy literato would call that animal you keep the Prince of Darkness, for he was a gentleman, as I remember.'

'I was bored,' said Donally. 'I was ambitious. I wanted to see the world.'

A draught made the flames of the candles dance and the air grew thick with the smell of hot wax. Marianne's eyes had grown more and more accustomed to the candlelight and she made out knobs and swags of carving in the ceiling, flowers, cherubs, jacks-in-the-green, death's heads, hourglasses and memento mori, all covered with dust. Trunks, chests and cases were littered everywhere, covered with dusty utensils and more books even than in her father's study. He must have a special cart to himself to transport them all. Yellow weeds blossomed in the walls and somewhere moisture dripped.

'Well, here you are at the end of the road, holed up in a ruin with your rotten library, aren't you?' she said nastily. 'Why did you never teach Jewel to read?'

'Self-defence, in the first instance,' he explained briskly. 'On the second count, I wanted to maintain him in a crude state of unrefined energy.'

'What, keep him beautifully savage?'

'Why, yes. Exactly,' said Donally. His eyelids fluttered; he continued to stroke his purple hairs with a fine, white hand, now contemplating Marianne as if she were a good deal more clever than he had ever suspected.

'Our Jewel is more savage than he is barbarous; literacy would blur his outlines, you wouldn't see which way he was going any more.'

The smells of hot wax and the vile brew he stewed on his stove combined to make Marianne dizzy, though Donally's voice and intonation were so familiar there was almost some comfort to be derived from them, though everything he said seemed wilfully perverse. When he moved, a faint perfume of lemon verbena drifted from his shirt, a clean, refreshing smell which cleared her head.

'Why have you only communicated with me so far by means of your nasty graffiti?'

'So nobody could hear what I was saying,' he replied. 'Besides, there's nothing much to do in the evenings except coin an aphorism or two.'

'I should have thought you were a man of many interests.'

'I run through the occasional fugue. And, then, I've my fits to practise, of course; I understand they're very impressive.'

'Also you cultivate your serpentarium,' she said. 'Jewel told me about your snake, unless I was imagining it.'

'It seemed to me that the collapse of civilization in the form that intellectuals such as ourselves understood it might be as good a time as any for crafting a new religion,' he said modestly. 'If they won't take to the snake for a symbol, we'll think of something else suitable, in time. I still use most of the forms of the Church of England. I find they're infinitely adaptable. Religion is a device for instituting the sense of a privileged group, you understand; many are called but few are chosen and, coaxed from incoherence, we shall leave the indecent condition of barbarism and aspire towards that of the honest savage, maintaining some kind of commonwealth. Let me give you a quotation.'

He riffled through a book sprouting with markers and found his place; he coughed and read aloud:

'The passion to be reckoned upon is fear; whereof there be two very general objects: one, the power of spirits invisible, the other, the power of those men they shall therein offend.'

'My father had that book,' said Marianne. 'Only he didn't like it much.'

'Doubtless he hoped for the best,' said Donally. 'He didn't have to create a power structure and fortify it by any means at his disposal. He was sustained by ritual and tradition; both of which I must invent. I think the wedding ceremony will be more impressive if it takes place at night. I have a very frightening dress for you to wear, all ready prepared. You have no choice at all, you know. It's marry or burn.'

He smiled at her again; then he took up his candle and walked briskly to the wall. Raising the candle, he illuminated a stone fissure so she could see within a grinning medieval skeleton who carried a stone banner engraved with the motto: AS I AM, SO YE SHALL BE. Marianne gave the Doctor a thin, pale smile and rushed headlong from the room, accompanied by the well-bred cadences of his laughter.

Outside in the brilliant sunshine, naked children played a game of tig along the terrace and through the rose garden. Marianne came out of the front door and a communal sigh went up. The children scattered at once but Mrs Green's granddaughter went down the stairs so fast she tripped and rolled head over heels to the bottom, where she lay yowling in a clump of long grass. Marianne went down the staircase, set the child upright and dusted earth from the wrinkles in her bare stomach. Jen scowled.

'I hope Jewel shows you what's what,' she said. 'I hope he beats you with his fists, once he's married to you.'

'News certainly travels fast,' said Marianne. 'Who told you he was marrying me?'

'I hope he keeps you in a cage, like that snake,' said the child. 'And I'll come and poke a stick through the bars.'

She squinted at Marianne malevolently and all at once lost interest. She stuck her dirty thumb in her mouth and wandered off, through the rose trees where her friends were playing a new game. The overblown, dishevelled roses cast down petals on all sides; in this romantic setting, the children pelted the half-witted boy with stones. He crouched under a white rose tree which, shaken by the frequent impact of the stones, snowed him with petals. He was protecting his eyes with his hands.

'I can see you!' snarled Marianne with considerable ferocity, parting the spiky branches and glaring at the children. Once again, they scattered and the boy collapsed, weeping, on his face.

She walked towards the river, across the meadow where ponies and horses were grazing. They raised their heads and fluttered their velvet nostrils at her; the gentleness of their eyes comforted her but the unnatural beauty of the valley made her sad, for the banners of purple loosestrife streaming from the roof in the sunshine were like the triumphant flags of nature herself, staking her claim to the building. She walked a little way up the river, towards the point where it disappeared into the woods, and saw Precious there. He had ridden a horse into the river, to water it. He wore hardly more clothes than the children did.

He did not see Marianne. His black hair hung down over his cheek, hiding the marks of the tattooing needle, and he twisted his fingers in the black mane of a bay horse and sang a very simple tune to himself; he repeated the tritonic phrase over and over again almost as though he had forgotten he were singing. The bones had not yet formed an implacable casque beneath the soft flesh of his face and his thin, brown, adolescent legs dangled against the pony's flank negligently. Precious had not finished growing. He waded downstream, the horse parted the reeds in the dark water and Marianne gasped, for the rider looked just as if he had come from the hands of original nature, an animal weaker than some and less agile than others, but, taking him all round, the most advantageously organized of any, pure essence of man in his most innocent state, more nearly related to the river than to herself. His eyes were closed, perhaps he was dreaming; but she could not conceive what dreams the Barbarians dreamed, unless she herself was playing a part in one of their dreams.

'I thought things would be more simple, among the Barbarians,' said Marianne to herself and all at once felt lonely.

'Why did you stay? Tell me the real reason,' she said to Mrs Green later, when they were in the kitchen by themselves and Mrs Green was heating water in a black iron pot, to wash Marianne with. Mrs Green tested the water with her elbow and smiled gently into its wrinkling surface where little bubbles were rising.

'They left the prints of the heels of their boots on my heart,' she said.

'I saw them first when I was a little girl. I saw them riding into the village and everyone was so frightened and one of them killed my brother but I could tell, even then, that a horseman had very little chance against a disciplined soldier.'

'Oh, they never win outright but, then, they don't need to, do they? Just a bit of pillaging to bring back what we need. The flour and so on.'

'Fear is their major weapon, so they need to get themselves up to look like nothing on earth, not men at all.'

'Oh, yes,' said Mrs Green. 'It's a right old raree show. Colourful.

You'd better wash down here and I'll stay by the door so that nobody comes in. You wouldn't want, say, Johnny to find you in your altogether.'

Marianne put the cauldron of water on the table and washed herself limb by limb. Mrs Green gave her a piece of soap she had secreted in the bottom of her trunk for years, in case of an occasion like this. The Barbarians made no soap themselves and rarely felt the need for it. As she washed her arms, the light in the kitchen darkened; looking up, she saw the half-witted boy, freed from his chain, sitting on the window ledge making signs and faces at her. She gave a little cry of surprise. Mrs Green was affronted and ran into the backyard to shoo him away. Marianne wrapped the skirt round herself and followed her; the boy was rolling on the ground and Mrs Green was trying to prise apart his fingers, which were tightly clasped around something he clearly did not wish to show her.

'It's for the Professor girl,' he said. 'It's a wedding present.'

'Here I am,' said Marianne, kneeling beside him.

He grew quiet at once and sat up on his haunches. His chain and collar hung threateningly from the kennel but someone had rubbed fat on the sore place in his neck. The boy giggled and shuddered, hiding his face with his paw, and pressed the contents of the other fist into Marianne's palm. The promised present comprised a few stalks of grass and some crumpled rose petals.

'Thank you,' said Marianne gravely, looking into his swimming eyes.

'It was the best I could manage, in the circumstances,' he said. His voice was as thin as his father's and his articulation surprisingly precise.

'Your father'll beat the daylights out of you if he finds you roaming loose.'

'He said I could go out, he was angry with Jewel for cutting the collar but he said I could go about loose because today was special and Jewel put grease on my sore because he said it was his wedding day.'

'Well . . .' said Mrs Green doubtfully, looking down at him in perplexity. 'You can't hang about looking through the windows, you know. You just lie down in your kennel like a good boy and I'll go and get you a bite to eat.'

He crawled into the kennel and sat down with a sigh on a heap of filthy straw.

'Can I have a bit of wedding cake, later?'

'There isn't any wedding cake, nowadays, there hasn't been any wedding cake for years and years and years. How the hell did you get to hear about wedding cake?'

'I don't know,' said the boy. 'Somewhere.'

He sighed gustily again and began to masturbate. This shocked Mrs Green, who went: 'Tsk, tsk,' and hastily shepherded Marianne back into the kitchen, where she finished washing in the cooling water.

'He's no idiot,' said Marianne. 'Certainly no more of an idiot than anyone would be who had always been kept tied up on the end of a chain.'

'He was ever so funny when he was a kid, drooling and that. And those fits, just like his dad, dreadful fits. Frothing at the mouth and gnashing his teeth. I hate to think what'll happen to him in a year or two, with the girls and that. They go out and play with him and tease him now, as it is; it's disgusting, and Donally beats him something dreadful, then, like it was his fault.'

She helped Marianne to dry herself and they went up to her room, where she lit the fire. A large metal box had been deposited on the floor in their absence.

'Is that my wedding dress in there?'

'I suppose so, dear.'

'And when does the ceremony begin?'

'About nightfall.'

Mrs Green produced her comb and began, unhappily, to comb Marianne's hair, which surreptitiously she had kept cropped for fear of vermin by nibbling away at it with a little knife.

'It's all wrong for a girl to have hair as short as you,' she said. 'Why ever did they do it to you?'

'I do it to myself.'

Mrs Green stared.

'You're an odd one, aren't you. You can't have fitted in.'

Marianne sat on the mattress with her arms locked around her knees, discontentedly contemplating whatever might happen to her next, for she had no control over it.

'Open the box, Mrs Green, let me see my dress.'

Mrs Green lifted the creaking lid of the metal chest and unfolded a great deal of thin, yellow paper that crumpled away to dust beneath her fingers. Scooping away the paper, she dug down and unearthed a wedding dress such as Marianne had only seen in surviving photographs of the time before the war. She left the bed and crept near the chest, staring at its contents with amazement and a certain distaste.

The dress had a satin bodice, now fissured with innumerable fine cracks; long, tight, white sleeves that came to a point over the backs of the hands and an endless skirt of time-yellowed tulle. There was a vast acreage of net veil and a small garland of artificial pearls. Most of the pearl coating had detached itself from the surfaces so they were now only little globes of white glass. Mrs Green laid the dress out on the bed with a bemused expression on her face. Marianne screwed up a handful of the hem and watched the fabric shiver to dust between her fingers, just as the paper had done. There were shadows of mildew in every fold of the voluminous skirt and all smelled musty and stale.

'How perfectly ludicrous!' said Marianne. She could not control her laughter and Mrs Green laughed, also, though with an undertone of disquiet.

'Oh, it'll make an impression,' she said. 'It's the kind of thing they think the Professors wear in the privacy of their own homes, you know.'

'It's far too big for me.'

'Nobody will notice. There's nothing else to compare it with. It'll just be generally impressive.'

'It's horrible and disgusting,' said Marianne. 'And probably full of germs, too.'

'Well, I don't know about that,' said Mrs Green. She lingered at the door. 'I've got to be going, dear, got to get ready a big meal, for afterwards.'

'Festivities,' suggested Marianne coldly. 'Rejoicings.'

'You just do what you're told, get that dress on and wait,' said Mrs Green angrily, her patience suddenly exhausted. 'I'll be back to fetch you when it's time.'

Marianne heard her shift the log of wood against the door and knew she was locked in again. She retreated to the fireside, as far away from the dress as she could get, for she could not help watching it. As the room grew dark, the dress took on a moon-like glimmer and seemed to send out more and more filaments of tulle, like a growth of pale fungus shooting out airy spores, a palpable white infection; viruses of plagues named after the labels on the test-tubes in which they had been bred might survive for years under the briars of a dead city, nesting invisibly in the contents of just such a Pandora's box as this metal chest, starred with singed stickers of foreign places dating from those times when foreign places had more than an imaginative existence, for where was Paris any more, where they had briefly worshipped the goddess Reason.

She recoiled from the dress. It became an image of terror. Some young woman had worn it before her for a wedding in the old style with cake, wine and speeches; afterwards, the sky opened an umbrella of fire. Marianne pressed herself against the wall, face down on the floor-boards, and screwed her eyes shut, clenching her fists, attempting to force herself into a condition of detachment menaced as she was by this crumbling anachronism. When the room was quite dark, the dress was still visible, glowing with the luminosity of hoar frost, or the green light of the evening star, and Mrs Green bustled back with a lamp.

She was flushed and breathless. She brought with her the sharp smell of burned fat and roasting meat. Her apron was splashed with dripping and her hair was coming loose from its coil.

'You should have put the dress on,' she said sharply.

She took up the dress, very tenderly, and approached Marianne, carrying it, with the heavy, inexorable tread of a determined old lady. Marianne knew there was nothing for it and she must undergo her ordeal; she began mechanically to unbutton her shirt. She was shaking and sweating but her ruling passion was always anger rather than fear and she turned into a mute, furious doll which allowed itself to be totally engulfed. The satin bodice slid down her flesh with sensations of slime and ice and the skirts rippled out in a friable lake for yards over the floor. But Mrs Green darted round her with pins and the veil finally concealed everything, even Marianne's face, so at last she was quite transformed, now a pale bundle of aged fabric that disintegrated in little spurts with every movement she made. The bodice crackled and snapped.

'They'll have to marry me very quickly or every stitch will come apart and the dress vanish altogether,' she said.

Mrs Green retreated to the other end of the room and looked Marianne's yellowish, drifting, spectral figure up and down. The veil shook out in baleful streamers; Marianne extended her small, white, living hand to restrain it.

'It's not really very nice, is it,' said Mrs Green. 'You could never call me a superstitious woman but even so . . .'

Marianne saw a stain on the satin sleeve, where the original bride had spilled something, perhaps some wine. And maybe this other girl had been happy when she wore this dress and spilled her wine. Marianne's hard anger began to melt a little; she was seized with sadness.

'Who do you think wore it first?' she asked and tentatively stroked the satin with her forefinger, almost gently, almost as if asking the dress to forgive her for disliking it so.

'That way lies madness,' said Mrs Green sententiously. 'Oh, hell, you'll make a show. What a show. He's got the room all ready, candles everywhere, flowers. The snake in its little cage, he puts it on show in a little cage, see.'

'Is it a phallic snake, tonight?' asked Marianne.

'I don't know anything about that,' said Mrs Green. She took off her dirty apron and unfastened her dress. Beneath it, she wore a decent, high-necked petticoat cut out of sheeting. She found a clean dress identical with the first one in her private trunk and put it on, smoothing out the fold marks with her fingers. She wound up her hair with the skill of long habit and then she was ready, though she looked sad at heart.

'I worked for the Professors till I was older than you are now and I always thought they were a heartless lot,' she said suddenly. 'Be good to my Jewel, be kind.'

'Kind?' exclaimed Marianne, bewildered. 'Kind?'

'There you are,' said Mrs Green with a victorious melancholy. 'You don't understand.'

'Just yesterday he jumped on me with appalling brutality, he has the hands of a butcher and eyes like trick mirrors that can see out but cannot be seen through. We have nothing whatever in common and now you tell me to be kind to him!'

'You don't understand at all,' repeated Mrs Green. 'Now, put on a

haughty face because they think you're something quite out of the
ordinary. Though perhaps you look quite haughty enough, as it is.'

Marianne gathered up her voluminous petticoats disdainfully; Mrs
Green's mouth was turned down in lines of disapproval but, all the
same, she felt sorry for Marianne and this offended her most of all.

The ancient chapel was full of wild people in rags and fur. Their
hoops, clasps and collars of glass, metal and bone caught the light of
hundreds of candles attached to the stonework, so many candles the
room was ablaze, everything visible, the flags, the organ, the carving,
the lectern, the altar covered with candles and roses, an effigy of a
woman in a blue robe made of coloured wax which had melted over
the years so she looked dropsical. Somebody had picked every rose in
the rose garden and brought them to the chapel; they lay about in dying
heaps. The atmosphere, compounded of unwashed flesh, roses and
candles, was solid as cheese. It seemed that every member of the tribe
was present and all were perfectly still and silent, the babies silent at
their mothers' breasts and children clinging to skirts and peering
through the wood of legs at this apparition of another world in a dress
as old as their misfortunes, picking its way delicately through them.
As soon as Marianne appeared, a susurration of clothing indicated that
everyone there except Jewel and his brothers was making the sign
against the evil eye.

She was prepared for the unexpected; even so, the bizarre phenomenon of Donally took her by surprise. He was perched on the altar like
a grotesque bird. He had donned a mask of carved wood painted with
blue, green, purple and black blotches, dark red spots and scarlet streaks
which covered all his face but for the bristling parti-coloured beard. He
was robed from head to foot in a garment woven from the plumage of
birds. In his arms, he carried a plastic and wire cage of the kind in which
budgerigars had been kept before the war. This was twined with plastic
flowers cracked with age and half-melted, and also ribbons and feathers
so the adder presumably inside could not be seen. She wondered if
Donally would conclude the ceremony by attaching the snake to her
breast, like Cleopatra's asp. This black fancy gripped her so tenaciously
she found the palms of her hands were sweating and wiped them
furtively on her net skirts. The texture of the rushes on the floor under

her bare feet seemed to her the most ancient sensation in the world, archaic as the taste of cold water.

The brothers stood in a body behind Donally. They were wholly barbarian as she had first seen the Barbarians, nightmare incarnate. Each was painted with black round the eyes, white on the forehead and mouth and red on the cheekbones. Their long hair was as intricately plaited and ringletted as the wigs worn by the kings of Ancient Egypt. They were lavishly garnished with jewellery, some of which was of gold and precious stones, grubbed for in the deepest of the ruins, tarnished or in part reburnished. The three youngest even seemed to be wearing some pieces of armour, of all things, but Jewel had on a stiff coat of scarlet interwoven with gold thread, perhaps once a bishop's possession; he was as strangely magnificent as an Antediluvian king or a pre-Adamite sultan. Donally must have been robbing museums; perhaps he had been a Professor of History.

There were gold braid and feathers in Jewel's hair and very long earrings of carved silver in his ears. Darkness was made explicit in the altered contours of his face. He was like a work of art, as if created, not begotten, a fantastic dandy of the void whose true nature had been entirely subsumed to the alien and terrible beauty of a rhetorical gesture. His appearance was abstracted from his body, and he was wilfully reduced to sign language. He had become the sign of an idea of a hero; and she herself had been forced to impersonate the sign of a memory of a bride. But though she knew quite well she herself was only impersonating this sign, she could not tell whether Jewel was impersonating that other sign or had, indeed, become it, for every line of his outlandish figure expressed the most arrogant contempt and it was impossible to tell whether or not this contempt was in his script.

'Dearly beloved,' began Donally in a fat voice. 'We are gathered together . . .'

And he might as well utilize the Book of Common Prayer as anything else, since whatever he said made no sense to the wild congregation who had ears only for his melodious and hieratic intonation. His voice issued with mysterious hollowness from behind the mask and the tribe sighed. Now Marianne was close to the cage, she could see the spotted snake was sleeping peacefully. The brothers stood still as figures painted on the wall of a cave and watched her. She was glad the veil hid her face. A child grew bored or scared and began to cry; some woman shushed it unsuccessfully and then led it out by the hand. When the door opened, the sudden draught lifted the veil and wafted it right over Donally, momentarily clinging to his wooden brow and feathered shoulders like a sudden snowfall.

Irritation checked his smooth, oratorial flow for a moment and he pettishly brushed the veil aside so that her own face was partly visible. Then Jewel had to lean across and marry her with the first ring he came to on his forefinger, a signet ring with a lock of hair from the head of some dead person set in it. This ring hung so loosely on the fourth finger of her left hand that he jammed it over her thumb, instead, bruising the joint; he looked up at her sharply, as if this gratuitous piece of symbolism annoyed him beyond belief. He caught sight of her face at a new angle, half in shadows; the opaque brown discs of his eyes opened up and, for the first time, transmitted a message to her, a sudden and horrified flash of recognition. He dropped her hand as if it burned him. Meanwhile, the service went on.

She found Donally had incorporated a piece of ritual of his own invention, perhaps derived from a study of the culture of the Red Indians. He spread out his arms and nodded his wooden head, emulating the preening of a winged serpent. His beautiful plumage looked now like feathers, now like scales. All at once, the tribe broke rank and surged up and around the altar to see whatever was going to happen next more clearly, though they left a copious safety margin around Marianne's dissolving perimeters. Jewel had closed his eyes so she could not see into them any more. Drops of sweat broke through the paint on his forehead. He took out and brusquely offered her the blade of his knife, as though to stab herself with it. She flinched involuntarily. His eyes snapped open; he grimaced and snatched at her hand. She writhed and struggled; she tried to shout but the drifting veil caught in her mouth and gagged her. Donally's talons gripped her arm and she ceased to struggle, helplessly gazing on as Jewel advanced the blade towards her wrist. He made a little cut in the flesh and a few drops of blood oozed out. She had expected far worse. It hardly hurt at all. There was a tremendous rush of expelled breath in the chapel to see how red her blood was.

Jewel handed his knife to Johnny, who slit his brother's wrist just as Jewel had slit Marianne's. Jewel was shaking so much the knife made a dangerous, jagged gash and blood gushed vigorously over his brown skin; she realized he was choking back a fit of hysterical laughter as Donally leaned ceremoniously forward to clasp their two wounds together so that their bloods could be seen to mix. A good deal of blood splashed over her dress. When this rite was satisfactorily accomplished and Jewel was holding back the blood with his free hand, Donally leaped high into the air, screamed loudly once and flung himself down among the rushes, frothing and babbling in a tremendous fit.

He rolled and tossed like a tumultuous river, blowing out an incoherent spume of sound. The tribe pressed back against the walls to allow him room. Many children burst into tears while their parents stared from eyes round with fright and awe. The fit encompassed as many baroque variations as if he were playing the organ and lasted until the candles were half burned down and the snake continued to sleep all the time, even when Donally rolled and jolted against the cage, so Marianne wondered if it were a real snake or perhaps only a stuffed skin.

Spent and exhausted, Donally lay in a heap of plumage. Feathers were shed all over the floor and there was a sense of equal exhaustion in the room, as though the tribe had suffered through his crazy encounter with chaos with him. When he was still at last, the final few twitches done with, the tribe filed slowly out of the room until only the bride and groom, the brothers and Mrs Green were left. The brothers now stood at ease, scratching themselves and yawning.

'My poor Jen,' said Mrs Green. 'She was wailing, ever-so.'

'Give us a bit of bandage before I bleed to death,' said Jewel. Mrs Green found a handkerchief and wrapped up his wrist.

'There's a feast,' he added, keeping his eyes on the bandaging. 'A wedding feast.'

The felled archaeopteryx on the floor reassembled itself briskly.

The table in the kitchen was spread with flat bread, joints of meat and jugs of the crude liquor they brewed themselves. Marianne tasted a little of it and spat it out. Dogs and babies jostled one another on the floor for tidbits while Marianne sat at one end of the table, carefully

arranged, laid out upright with the veil thrown back so they could all
see her face, and Jewel sat at the other. He fed the food from his plate
to a puppy and drank. The red and gold coat formed angular, sculptural
folds at his arms; he was like a king on a playing card. When he sensed
Marianne's eyes upon him, he turned away from her and gripped the
edge of the table so hard his knuckles went whiter than his own white
paint.

Donally flitted around the table shedding fluff and feathers, smiling,
chatting and joking; he had left his mask in the chapel and, with it, his
wizardry. He created, as from thin air, a festive board and in his benign
presence the Barbarians became simple peasants celebrating any wedding
at any time, by the light of a great fire. The mood was thick and coarse.
Later, there was music. Donally took up a fiddle and an old man played
a mouth-organ. Two or three children had jews' harps, which they
twanged against their teeth. There was dancing. The brothers shone like
dark fire and the shining pieces of metal with which they were decorated
sent coruscating reflections of light spinning over the walls, though the
eldest brother sat as if lost for ever in the scarlet recesses of his coat. He
was a coloured structure and, the coat opened, might reveal only the
lining of its own back, no body inside.

'You must go to bed,' said Mrs Green to Marianne. 'Have a drop
more to drink. You must go where Jewel sleeps.'

'Will they all come with me to see that justice is done?'

Mrs Green peered at her, bewildered, and shook her head.

'No, dear, they'll leave you quite alone. What do you expect, a
procession?'

'I'm prepared for anything,' said Marianne.

Jewel had found a room for himself high in the oldest part of the
house. Through a low arch at the end of a long corridor above the
chapel, Marianne found herself in a tower. A spiral staircase wound up
and up; the treads were obliquely worn with age and very steep, she
clung to the wall for safety as she followed Mrs Green's guttering lamp.
There was no other light. Rooms even the Barbarians left empty opened
on either side of the staircase, full of cold, stagnant air; and now the
fabric shuddered beneath their feet and she felt the walls grow moist
and mossy. Now and then her hands encountered a knot of dripping

plants. Her bare feet touched all manner of wet, unseen things. Higher and higher they went, the lamp revealing only black stone before, behind and all around.

'This place can't be safe in a wind,' observed Marianne.

'Ah, but it's private,' said Mrs Green. 'Grant him that.'

Marianne could almost feel the wind beneath her feet. It was like climbing up to the moon. At last they reached a little door, so low Marianne had to stoop, and they entered Jewel's room. It seemed he preferred the open air, for much of the roof had fallen in, revealing a large expanse of rich, blue, night sky scattered with a handful of stars. Mrs Green put down the lamp on a wooden box which stood against a wall and, when the wick steadied, Marianne saw surroundings already half given over to the forest.

A red berry blown by the wind or dropped from the beak of a bird had rooted in a corner and grown into a small but sturdy holly bush which spread healthy branches hung with all of Jewel's collection of necklaces he was not at that moment wearing, several items of clothing and a quantity of knives. The floor was littered with rubble, fallen tiles and a drifting tide of crisp dead leaves of many years, but enough of the floor had been cleared away to make room for a mattress heaped with furs for a primitive bride-bed and the wooden box, on which stood some little jars, a bowl of water, a towel, a gap-toothed comb and a razor. The old fireplace had been put back in order, for some sticks of dry wood were laid ready to burn in it. By a whim of chance, the heavy glass in the single, arched, tiny window had remained intact and Jewel had rubbed it clean, for some reason. Marianne saw the pale curve of a crescent moon above the forest through the window. Far away from the kitchen and the celebrating parts of the house, the wind whispered and murmured around the roof and she heard the heavy rattle of mice in the walls.

Mrs Green took a light from the lamp and lit the fire. Marianne bathed her cut wrist in the ferociously cold water; her blood, or Jewel's, she could not tell which, eddied out in pale streaks but the wound itself had closed up. Mrs Green took the veil from her head and bundled it up.

'Burn it,' said Marianne.

'It will set fire to the chimney.'

'Burn it!'

Mrs Green shrugged and thrust the veil into the hearth, where it blazed up immediately and then subsided in a glowing network of ashes. Marianne stepped gladly out of the wreckage of the wedding dress and they burned that, also. The skirt vanished up the chimney in big, flaring rags and blackly collapsed while the little glass globes which had once been pearls rolled hither and thither among the flames like distressed insects. Then it was all gone and Mrs Green poked the unrecognizable fragments with a stick. Marianne shivered with cold. She saw Mrs Green had spread out one of her own nightdresses for her on the bed, a voluminous shroud of flannel with lace around the neck. She put it on.

'The mixing of bloods, they didn't tell me about that. I didn't know they were going to do that. It upset me, you know, it did, really. What does he think he's on at?'

'I'm sure it was very impressive.'

'Oh, no doubt. But you can go too far.'

'I thought he was going to kill me, cut me up, fry me and distribute me in ritual gobbets to the tribe.'

'Did you really?' said Mrs Green, aghast. 'Oh, that couldn't happen here, not while the Bradleys still rule the roost.'

Marianne took a rug from the bed, dropped it by the fire and knelt on it, warming her cold hands at the flames.

'Jewel is drunk,' she said.

'Oh, yes,' said Mrs Green as though it were inevitable. 'He's in a horrible mood, as well. My poor boy, my poor boy's got a chronic gift for unhappiness.'

'Don't get maudlin, you silly old woman. That's the way mothers used to get at weddings; they always became sentimental, it was a tradition.'

She realized these words had accidentally conjured up the ghost of her own mother, who died for love of an only son, and she grew silent, fingering the fringes of the fur, rabbitskin or bunny. She kept a rabbit in a hutch and fed it with dandelion leaves, when she was four years old, before the Barbarians came; when she was a child, encapsulated in a safe, white tower with unreason at bay outside, beyond the barbed wire, a community so rational that when her white rabbit died they cut it open to find out why.

'My mother always loved my brother best,' she said vaguely to Mrs Green who stood beside her staring at the fire with a face furrowed by unguessable worries. Marianne moved closer to her for comfort, though she did not know how Mrs Green could comfort her except by the repetition of certain old saws about human behaviour which might or might not any longer have application.

The wick of the little lamp slumped beneath the fat and the flame was extinguished. Firelight filled the room. The door crashed back on its hinges and the delicately balanced room shuddered as if about to cast its moorings and plunge from the top of the tower. Jewel had arrived. He dragged the scarlet coat on the floor behind him, it was already very dirty. He shed it on a pile of rubble. He did not acknowledge the presence of his bride or foster-mother but went to dip his face in the bowl of water; he shook out a cascade of water drops and wiped himself with the towel. Marianne thought all his features might come off with the paint and he would raise a smooth, eyeless egg of flesh towards her but, in fact, he was himself again, if this was himself, though streaked and sullen. He emanated disquiet. Mrs Green got to her feet nervously.

'I'll be going, then,' she said.

Jewel said nothing. He took the silver earrings from his ears and dropped them on the floor. Marianne sat upright, bristling; some kind of electric charge filled the air, he sparked off antagonism and she began to enjoy herself. The dead leaves shifted about on the floor. Mrs Green took a brand from the fire to light her way downstairs; she glanced anxiously at the young man and young woman who glared at one another balefully and, huffing and puffing miserably, she took herself off. The door closed on her with a reverberating thud and a necklace of silver coins fell from the tree. Marianne decided to begin an offensive.

'What a farce,' she said as unpleasantly as she could. 'How grotesque.'

He grunted and tried to revive the lamp but failed. Accompanied by a faint tintinnabulation of jewellery, he approached the fire and, ignoring her, sat down cross-legged at the far end of the fur, all hunched up. He attempted to unwind his intricate fleece but his fingers fumbled and the knots of the leather thongs had jammed like rusty locks.

'Comb me,' he ordered and she was pleased to see intense hostility in his face.

She took the comb from the wooden box and knelt down with a certain derision, freeing the hair from its myriad of little plaits. But she could not deny that he looked marvellously exotic, with grains of black paint in the corners of his eyes, eyes with extraordinarily heavy lids. As she continued with her task, tension diminished; it was an action altogether out of time, something she would never have believed possible for herself and, as she felt the dry, gleaming weight of his endless black hair slide through her fingers, the repetition and intimacy of her movements and the strangeness of the events of the day combined almost to subdue her. The acrid woodsmoke made her eyes smart and the glossy leaves of the tree in the corner shone like looking-glass, high in the sky above the world, and she felt a tranced bewilderment. She realized she was very tired.

When the plaits were undone, she continued mechanically to comb the amazing black waterfall, coarse and straight as horse-hair, and he moved a little under her touch, as if in recognition of the involuntary sensuality that caused her hand to move more and more slowly, with more and more dreamy a rhythm. The loose ring rolled off her thumb and away across the floor; this hushed chink was enough to wake her and, deliberately, she clasped her arms around the man's neck and pressed his face into her breast, for she could not bear to wait any longer for something to happen.

He had also been waiting for something to happen. As if he expected her to embrace him all the time, he at once caught hold of her wrists and bent her backwards until she was stretched out on the skin rug with her arms pinned down to the floor behind her head. The brown man arched above her; he said: 'I hate you.'

She was neither surprised nor shocked. If she had thought about it, she would have anticipated something like this reaction and, if he had said anything else under the circumstances, she would have been quite terrified, not knowing what to do. As it was, she waited calmly for him to release his hold. She inspected the hard jewel of dry blood on the inside of his forearm and a blue enamel pendant, a St Christopher medallion, now secular decoration unless he wore it for the travelling, which hung from his neck among a shifting mass of glass beads.

'I hate you,' he repeated in a very soft voice. An owl hooted and a horse neighed; outside, and very faintly, she heard a woman scream and then laugh.

'Why?' she asked curiously, for she was very interested.

'Because, because, because . . .' He let go of her and sat upright again as if he had never moved at all, covering his face with his hands. She rubbed her wrists.

'Because of your traditional hatred, dating back to the time of the deep shelters?'

He shook his head.

'Because I'm cleverer than you?'

Stung, he replied: 'I think that's most unlikely,' and relapsed again into silence.

'You're drunk,' she said angrily. 'Go to bed, go on; tell me in the morning.'

'Come on, now,' he said. 'You can read, read me. I've seen you before, before you rescued me.'

He pushed back his hair as if presenting her his face displayed upon a platter, a face which at that moment appeared of such desolate beauty so far from the norm it was as fearful as a gross deformity. Her heart sank and she recognized him, though he had completely changed.

'You were much younger, then,' she said. 'And looked more like Precious than yourself.'

'I was fifteen, yes.'

'It was my brother you killed.'

'I expect so, yes.'

'I remember everything perfectly.'

'You've disguised yourself cunningly, haven't you, cutting off your hair and all. Who'd have thought I ever could recognize you, unless what I thought was true, that this child who looked so severe would be the death of me.'

Marianne retreated from him backwards, across the room, until she found herself in the jewelled arms of the tree.

'What ice-water eyes you have,' he said. He pulled a knife from his belt and threw it at her; she caught it by the handle. He fell backwards on the rug, tore open his shirt and offered her his bared breast.

'Shall you kill me now or later?' he asked.

'Whichever you prefer,' said Marianne impatiently.

She dropped the knife on the floor for she had no desire to kill him; after her first shock of surprise, she felt no desire for revenge, either, only an angry disquiet, as if he had broken into her most private place and stolen her most ambiguously cherished possession. Her memory was no longer her own; he shared it. She had never invited him there. Yet the thing that happened one May Day under her balcony seemed to have very little to do with either of them, since now she was a different person and currently pretending to be the memory of a bride. And, since she and the murderer were now incarnated as bride and groom, she felt the only action available to them was to go to bed together, according to the prescribed ritual. She came out of the shadow of the indoor branches, cool again.

'You don't believe in your own magics but you believe those of other people,' she said in a very cruel voice. 'I don't think you're clever at all.'

He stopped lying on the floor and, instead, crouched defensively.

'I'm frightened of what I don't know about,' he said. 'That seems reasonable to me.'

'Well, you needn't be frightened of me. You've made me bleed twice, no, three times already; you're much stronger than I and, as far as it goes, more powerful –'

Then addressing words shaped by reason, no matter how roughly shaped, to the piece of darkness crouched beside the dying fire in the unlit room seemed to her so futile a task she stopped speaking in mid-sentence, gathered her engulfing nightdress around her and stalked to the mattress. She lay down between the covers. Hay rustled beneath her.

'This little girl, she was about Jen's age, looking down as if it were all an entertainment laid on for her benefit. And I thought, "If that's the way they look at death, the sooner they all go the better."'

She closed her eyes briefly.

'Please stop. Please come to bed.'

'The death of me,' he repeated very softly.

'You are very superstitious and very drunk,' said Marianne austerely, determined to put an end to this. 'I am only in your bed by accident, anyway. It's your good fortune if this accident happens to serve you as a focus for your moral guilt.'

He shrieked with uncontrollable laughter, coughed for a few minutes, and then sat smarting with miserable fury.

'She keeps her flag flying,' he addressed the tree. 'She keeps utilizing her perceptions until the very end.'

He rose to his knees and stretched his arms towards her.

'Lead me by the hand. Lead me to the gates of paradise.'

'Why are you putting me through this ordeal by imagery?'

'Didn't they use to wear black gloves at funerals? Donally must have shown me a picture. I always think of death as wearing black gloves but nobody wears them any more.'

'Are you coming to bed or are you going to sleep on the floor?'

'Lead me. Come on.'

She realized she would never get any sleep that night unless she brought him to the bed herself. But she saw with irritation and some perturbation that now he appeared an almost infinitesimal figure beside a fire at the other side of a hundred miles of yielding floorboards and heaped debris as of a battlefield. The room was growing very dark. She reluctantly got up from the mattress. Draughts played across the floor and blew her nightdress about. Any moment the room might blow away altogether and go whirling off through the night; or else it was being blown up like a huge balloon to become a round world itself, he at one pole and she at the other. It seemed to take hours to cross the floor and when she at last arrived beside him, they clutched one another's hands with almost the same kind of terrified relief. She pulled him upright in an echoing jangle of jewellery.

'Charms and amulets to keep away wild beasts, devils and sicknesses,' he said. 'To deflect the arrows of the Out People, the bullets of the Professors and who knows what else.'

He supported himself on her shoulder and scattered chains and necklaces about the floor. It was now very cold. Rings fell down from his fingers like a brilliant hail and she led him to the mattress. His clothes followed the jewellery; he left behind a trail of shed clothing until he was as naked as the day he was born. They moved out of the last red light of the fire into the deepening shadows; when she got him under the covers, she could no longer see where the darkness ended and his body began.

'I'm too drunk to screw you,' he said.

'One must be thankful for small mercies,' she snapped. He laughed with apparently genuine delight.

'Wit,' he acknowledged. 'Not very polished but, all the same, wit. A joke. We don't have much time to practise that kind of thing.'

So they effected a truce. He threw his arms across her, perhaps for warmth, perhaps for peacefulness if not reconciliation, but, in any case, they both went to sleep immediately out of gratitude that the room had returned to its ordinary dimensions. But as soon as night started to roll back its heavy carpet and dawn came through the roof, she opened her eyes and found he was already awake, leaning over her and looking at her with assessment and surmise. She thought: 'Perhaps my father was right, perhaps chaos is even more boring than order.' She hoped she was dreaming him but one cannot dream the sensation of another person's body heat. His body heat suffused her.

'I thought you'd sleep late,' she said.

'Wrong again,' he retorted. 'I was tormented by the nightmare. I habitually sweat beneath her till day-break, no matter what.'

'What do you dream of?'

'Fires and knives.'

'I don't dream at all,' said Marianne truculently. 'Or, if I do, I never remember them.'

'Then aren't you the lucky one. However, I daresay you're lying.'

She moved uneasily under the absolute intensity of his gaze and at last admitted:

'Well . . . when I was a little girl, I used to dream about the Barbarians and that used to disturb me, but never to the point of sweating and moaning. At least, not often. And then it was never out of fear.'

'Sometimes I dream I am an invention of the Professors; they project their fears outside on us so they won't stay in the villages, infecting them, and so, you understand, they can try to live peacefully there. On the nights I have these dreams, I have been known to wake the entire camp with my screams.'

The dawn came into the room by two routes, flooding through the ceiling and edging more timorously through the window. They lay upon the narrow mattress and, involuntarily, by a compulsion that had nothing to do with reason, will or conscious desire, she found she moved closer and closer to him. He was a curiously shaped, attractive stone; he was an object which drew her. She examined the holes pierced in his ears to contain earrings. She had read such cool words in the books in her father's study and looked there at line diagrams of segmented forms stuck with arrows tipped with frozen words in dead languages; she had heard her father's gentle voice speaking of happenings between men and women that, in spite of her affection, she could not associate with happenings between the hairless old man and her mother's ghost; now she lay far away from his white tower with a beautiful stranger beside her and he stark naked.

'Why are you crying?'

'I was thinking about my father.'

As if he absorbed all the atmosphere, she found it difficult to breathe. Nothing she had yet seen or suffered of him could prevent her insensibly moving still closer; a bird flew down through the roof and perched on a branch above a string of pearls. It fluttered its wings and let out a little rippling run of song. She was filled with astonishment that the room contained the world or the world had become only the room; she put her arms around him and caressed him. Her movement startled the bird, it flew away. Searching for her complementary zones, he pushed the overwhelming folds of his foster-mother's nightdress up around her waist. She pulled the nightdress over her head and threw it away, so she could be still closer to him or, rather, to the magic source of attraction constituted by his brown flesh. And, if anything else but this existed, then she was sure it was not real.

'She's given you her best nightdress; she always told me to lay her out in that.'

If, the night before, his face had been a construct of paint and shadow, now it was entirely bone again and she got no messages whatsoever from his eyes. Perhaps he was trying to make friends with her or perhaps he was trying to learn her. There was no pain this time. The mysterious glide of planes of flesh within her bore no relation to anything she had heard, read or experienced. She never expected such extreme intimations of pleasure or despair. If he was surprised at her response, he kept it to himself but when he withdrew he remained lying across her, covering her, still fixing her with this same, assessing regard as though he were trying to see the web of tissue and muscle behind her eyes, or even more of her interior than that. As they lay clasped together in this fashion, the door opened and Mrs Green came in carrying a dish in her hands. She placed this dish on the box where the bowl of water stood and bent to gather Jewel's scattered clothing from the floor.

'I'm glad you're getting on so well,' she said, glancing at them. Her voice was warm with contentment. Marianne was disconcerted and turned her flushed face into the furs but Jewel appeared unmoved. He shifted slowly away from her, accepted a handful of rings from his foster-mother and slid them on his fingers, one on each finger, two on some. It was full morning and the room had become a dazzling bubble of sunshine and air. Mrs Green pointed to the dish.

'I brought you some breakfast,' she said. 'I thought that would be nice. It's, you know, all right.'

'What do you mean?' asked Marianne, puzzled, surfacing from the covers.

Mrs Green set her hands on her hips. Her soft, white face took on as inscrutable an expression as any Barbarian born.

'He came padding downstairs early in the morning, unlike him, and he gave me a little bottle of stuff and told me to feed it to the happy couple as he called them, so they would have many children, see. He must have thought I was soft, dear. I fed some of the stuff to the brown bitch's puppy and it ran round in circles till it dropped down dead.'

When she heard this, Marianne felt so cold she thought the sun had gone in and she crept back into Jewel's arms but Mrs Green and he burst out laughing.

'He's losing his subtlety, poor old sod,' said Jewel. 'He's getting old.'

'I suppose he'd have said the girl poisoned you.'

'I daresay.'

While Marianne stared from one to the other, trying to discover the reason for their amusement, Mrs Green bent down and ripped the furs off them.

'Look at him, isn't he a lovely boy? If I was thirty years younger . . .'

'Forty years,' said Jewel. 'Don't let's exaggerate.'

He pushed Marianne to one side, threw his arms round the old woman's neck, drew her down to him and kissed her, laughing. Marianne watched them, leaning on her elbow, colder than ever; then she saw an extraordinary pattern on Jewel's back, flickering through the black river of his hair, a pattern of as many colours as *Viperus berus* in his cage in Donally's room. At first she thought this must be the symptom of some extraordinary disease, no doubt connected with his fits of coughing, and reached out to touch it but Jewel was collecting the porridge bowl and pushed her away again. He scooped up a little of the thin, grey, viscous substance with his fingers and said to Marianne: 'Look at me carefully and, if I swell up and die, don't eat anything but go to Johnny directly and tell him to look after you.'

'Don't tease her.'

Jewel ate, did not die and passed the food to her. She did not want to eat, she put the bowl down on the floor beside her.

'Give us my shirt,' he said to Mrs Green. 'I'd better be up since I've lived to see another day.'

On her way to the door, Mrs Green threw him his shirt.

'Is she going to stay with me today or what's she going to do; we'll have to find something for her to do.'

'She'll do what she wants.'

Mrs Green nodded and went out; the closing of the door dislodged a fresh piece of roof into the room and every bird in the world sang outside.

'Don't put your shirt on, yet – turn round. No, lie down again. On your face.'

He raised his eyebrows but obeyed her. She parted the black curtains of his mane and drew her hands incredulously down the ornamented length of his back. He wore the figure of a man on the right side, a woman on the left and, tattooed the length of his spine, a tree with a snake curled round and round the trunk. This elaborate design was executed in blue, red, black and green. The woman offered the man a red apple and more red apples grew among green leaves at the top of the tree, spreading across his shoulders, and the black roots of the tree

twisted and ended at the top of his buttocks. The figures were both stiff
and lifelike; Eve wore a perfidious smile. The lines of colour were etched
with obsessive precision on the shining, close-pored skin which rose
and fell with Jewel's breathing, so it seemed the snake's forked tongue
darted in and out and the leaves on the tree moved in a small wind, an
effect the designer must have foreseen and allowed for.

'Oh, yes,' said Jewel. 'I understand that's very impressive.'

He put on his shirt and covered up the grotesque disfigurement,
which fascinated her. Even their wedding breakfast of poisoned porridge
was less remarkable to her than this close undergarment of colour.

'You can never take all your clothes off,' she said. 'Or be properly by
yourself, with Adam and Eve there all the time.'

'Out of sight is out of mind,' said Jewel. 'I've never seen it, it being
on my back. He called it his masterpiece, he did it when I was fifteen.'

'Was it very painful?'

'He took a fortnight and I was delirious most of the time but the
needles didn't poison my blood because Mrs Green looked after them.
Though green, in fact, is the worst, green hurts most of all. You'll notice
what a lot of green there is in the picture.'

He got up and put on his trousers. Then his boots. The concealing
shirt. Then sorted necklaces from the heap on the rug. He was putting
his daytime self together.

'He wanted to do the Last Judgement on my chest, but I didn't want
nothing I could see all the time, did I.'

'Is he very fond of the Bible?'

'When pressed, he'll talk about the poetic truth of the legend of the
Fall of Man.'

'Why did you let him mutilate you so?'

'Do you see it as a mutilation?' He was engaged in plaiting his hair.

'It's hideous. It's unnatural.' But she was lying again; the tattoo
seemed to her a perilous and irresistible landscape, a terra incognita or
the back of the moon.

'From time to time, he makes me take off my shirt for him and he
prowls round admiring me, saying: "Ha, hum, what genius I had then."
I think he'd like to flay me and hang me up on the wall, I think he'd
really like that. He might even make me up into a ceremonial robe and

wear me on special occasions. He tattooed some little girl all over with
tiger stripes, once, and said she'd be the Tiger Lady. But she died, it was
a failure.'

'Why did you allow him to attack you with his needles?'

'I didn't have much choice. I was only a kid.'

'I do not like it here,' she said disapprovingly. 'I do not like it at all.'

She sat up straight, formal and prim, with her hands around her
knees and the furs in a shawl around her shoulders. He looked at her
with something like nostalgia, as if she were an old photograph.

'Poor kid,' he said. 'And there I was, afraid of you.'

'Please will you go away and leave me alone, now,' she said for he
had taken on in her eyes the ghastly attraction of the deformed and she
needed time for introspection on this account.

He gave her his vilest, snarling grin, paused as in thought and then
returned to where she lay. He kissed her breasts and mouth for several
minutes and left her alone, after that, accompanied only by her newly-
awakened, raging and unsatisfied desire, another indignity heaped upon
her she vengefully added to the score.

Donally had written on his wall: MEMORY IS DEATH. Marianne
studied this for a long time, while the wall itself shivered from a furious
assault on the baroque organ behind it which was undergoing a toccata
fit to bring the house down. She thought of asking Donally to tattoo
this slogan across her forehead, where Jewel could see it all the time, or
else to tattoo: MEMORY on one of her breasts and: DEATH on the other.
But she soon thought better of this plan when she remembered that
Jewel had never learned to read.

5

The tribe no longer protected itself against Marianne with signs, for marriage had secularized her. She was still a stranger and hence fearful but now she was specifically Jewel's responsibility and evidently they trusted him to control her dubious magics, keeping them knotted in a bag, perhaps, under his pillow, for now the children were content to ignore her and she could come and go about the camp as she pleased, creating no ripples about her. When she asked for a pony, they gave her a little, black and white dappled one like a toy horse in a nursery, with a coarse white mane. Sometimes she rode around in the edges of the wood but went no farther. Time passed and Jewel watched her from the corners of his eyes but still she did not load up her pony and ride away for, as soon as she and the young man found out how to annihilate one another, she was unable to think of anything else for long. Courting her own extinction as well as his, she discovered extraordinary powers as soon as the dark removed the dangerous evidence of Jewel's face. Then their bed became a cold, black, silent world and its sole inhabitants were denied all other senses but those of touch, taste and smell.

But once she woke before him and was surprised to see his face quite reduced to gentleness. His hands had fallen upon her breasts as soft as snow in the abandonment of sleep and then, with fascinated horror, she revived the memory that these same hands which, a few hours previously, had temporarily altered her to a river of fire, also, a few years previously, had irrevocably murdered the flesh of her flesh. Jewel's face seemed to whirl about in the tense hollow of her shoulder, scatter and come together again in shapes of perfect fear; but he opened his eyes and suddenly she saw herself reflected twice, so quickly she turned her head away, before she could make out the expression she herself wore.

Another time, she woke in the middle of the night because a night-jar, come to perch on the tree in the room, whirred extremely loudly. It was the time of the month when there was no moon. She felt her eyes had been put out and, as she groped for Jewel's hand to prove she was not there all by herself, she encountered, by accident, his face. She touched a promontory of bone very lightly padded with flesh, which must be his cheekbone. She moved the whorled tips of her fingers lightly across this ridge and found a fringe as of grass, presumably an eye hooded under an eyelid. But she had no sense of real eyes or a real face under her fingers. All seemed a small landscape from which she received only the most abstract information and she soon identified this landscape with the blasted heart of the old city; this puzzled her a little but she refused to think about it for long.

Again, accidentally, afterwards, some other night, moving uneasily, she touched his face and found it was wet with tears. But he stayed still, sleeping or pretending to sleep, and she instantly repressed her curiosity.

Apart from these stray contacts, she defended herself by denying him an existence outside the dual being they made while owls pounced on velvet mice in the forest, the moon passed through its phases and the idiot boy howled disconsolately in his kennel. This third thing, this erotic beast, was eyeless, formless and equipped with one single mouth. It was amphibious and swam in black, brackish waters, sub-sisting only upon night and silence; she closed her eyes in case she glimpsed it by moonlight and there were no words of endearment in common, anyway, nor any reason to use them. The beast had teeth and claws. It was sometimes an instrument solely of vengefulness, though often its own impetus carried it beyond this function. When it separated out to themselves, again, they woke to the mutual distrust of the morning.

In daylight or firelight, she saw him in two dimensions, flat and effectless. When he came riding across the meadow on his black horse, soaked with rain or spattered with mud or blood, returning from the hunt; or waiting for the evening meal in the kitchen with his brothers, playing the game with bones and quarrelling sullenly about the fall of the pieces; or, occasionally, domestic, cradling furry Jen on his knee when she went to sleep there, as she sometimes did – all these activities were no more than sporadic tableaux vivants or random poses with no thread of continuity to hold them together.

On the wall outside the Doctor's room was written up: OUR NEEDS BEAR NO RELATION TO OUR DESIRES. He let it stay there for several weeks.

'But how can one tell which is which,' Marianne asked herself and thought no more about the slogan.

Marianne sat white and silent on the broken chair in the kitchen and sometimes sounds of organ music flitted around like baroque spooks and sometimes they did not. One evening, Jewel broke every pot on the old dresser in an outburst of rage. He hurled the antique crockery around the room; his brothers fled, helter-skelter, giggling with fear, but Marianne did not bother to move from her seat. He threw a soup tureen at her; it missed, of course, since neither it nor he were real. It crashed into the fire. He also began to attack the slaughtered carcasses with remarkable ferocity and, another evening, silently approached her during the butchery hour and daubed her face with his bloody hands, an action she construed immediately and immediately despised, as if he were helplessly trying to prove his autonomy to her when she knew all the time he vanished like a phantom at daybreak, or earlier, at the moment when her body ceased to define his outlines.

Sometimes, when it rained, rain drove across the room and soaked them to the skin. On windy nights, the room tossed like a cork upon stormy breakers of air. Every morning, a little more of the roof had fallen in, until they would soon be as cruelly exposed as babies on a mountain side and, each night, the spiral staircase grew a little more treacherous. Once she trod on a toad on her way to bed and broke its back.

Meanwhile, the tribe prepared to raise camp and move on. They made repairs to their carts and shod the horses. Jewel had inherited an affinity for horses from his mother's side, the Lees, but all the brothers looked very beautiful among the horses and Marianne inspected these sights as if she were looking at colour illustrations in an ingenious book. So at all times she maintained a triumphant loneliness in this strange place where she found herself.

She lived in this disintegrated state for some time, until, prone under his weight, she heard him growl into her throat: 'Conceive, you bitch, conceive' and was shocked into the most lucid wakefulness, so their connexion seemed all at once grotesque and brutal and the spurt of seed a terrible violation of her privacy. She never once, had thought the fish of night might achieve a concrete symbol, a child inside her; if she had ever idly considered it, she would have hoped their breeds were so far apart a cross would not have been possible. She desperately looked for him but could not see him for it was another night without a moon. So she had to speak to him at last.

'Why?'

He was silent so long she began to wonder if she had actually spoken aloud.

'Dynastically,' he said at last. 'It's a patriarchal system. I need a son, don't I, to dig my grave when I'm gone. A son to ensure my status.'

'Give me another reason.'

'Politically. To maintain my status.'

'I suppose these are both good reasons, given the initial situation, but I think there is a less abstract one.'

'Revenge,' he explained. 'Shoving a little me up you, a little me all furred, plaited and bristling with knives. Then I should have some status in relation to myself.'

'By submitting me to the most irretrievable humiliation. By making me give birth to monsters?'

'What, like the sleep of reason?'

'You're very sophisticated,' she complained.

'I do the best I can,' he returned politely.

She turned on her side and listened to the sounds of the night, nothing more than a small wind with a few drops of rain on it.

'And I saved your life, as well,' she said reproachfully.

'I shall give you another one.'

A flurry of rain pattered against the glass of the window and down on the hard leaves of the holly bush. Only the thinnest corroded shell of brick and slate protected them from the cold summer's night and the black deeps of sky. Rain blew into her face and settled on her cheeks. The idea of pleasure died now she realized pleasure was ancillary to procreation. When he reached out for her, she twisted away, disgusted.

'Go to sleep, then,' he snarled.

But now the room was full of faces floating bodiless on darkness like cream on milk, faces of diseased children shrieking raucously from warped mouths that she was their mother. The bed became hateful to her and the moisture seeping between her thighs some vile, powerful witch ointment which would send its victim mad. What was left of the roof would shortly cave in and bury them for ever in the infernal pit of their embraces; she choked on the stale air as if already buried alive. In fear and trembling, she slithered from the covers on to the floor, suddenly determined to be gone. Jewel was asleep, so far as she could tell. She dressed herself quickly in her Barbarian clothes, the only ones she had, now, trousers, a woollen shirt embroidered with daisies and little chips of mirror and a jacket of grey squirrel fur fastened at the throat with a diamanté brooch scavenged from some grave. She made her way to the door by touch and feel; underfoot was rubble and holly leaves. Jewel was not asleep.

'It's raining. You can't go now.'

'I can and will.'

'You might be incubating my child already. It's some time since I've been doing you.'

'The Professors know cures for that particular malady.'

'Take a knife. To protect yourself.'

'I'm not particularly afraid.'

'Not so much for the wild beasts. I only ever saw a lion once, in a wood. It lay across the carcass of a cow, beside the place where a train crashed, ooh, years ago, when they still had them. All the doors of this train were hanging down like the wings of a dead insect with ever so many wings and the lion had a bloody mouth. Also, gum seeped from its eyes. It was the colour of bracken and it got on with its dinner without minding me.'

'You are trying to appeal to my romanticism,' she said angrily. 'I'm not a child, to be taken in with pretty stories.'

'The wild beasts won't jump you but, on the other hand, the ruins are full of such horrors as lepers, madmen, hermits, men with heads of apes or single eyes in the middle of their foreheads, to say nothing of roving bands of Out People –'

'Goodbye,' she said crisply for, after all, he was her husband and deserved the formality of a farewell. But he did not say goodbye to her, even though she was his wife. Descending from the rickety tower, she sightlessly followed the inward spiral of the staircase and the only clue she had to guide her were her five fingers against the clammy surfaces of the walls. She inched her way gingerly, slithering on steps that had never before seemed so steep, so uncertain or so curded with slime, and the wind blew in fitful gusts, shaking the stones. The sickly air of the long corridor above the chapel struck surprisingly warm when at last she gained it. She made her way along this corridor and reached the landing where the chapel was; and Donally was waiting for her in the dark.

She was so angry with herself for not having guessed he would be waiting for her that she could not speak. She could see nothing of him at all but he closed his hand around her wrists and she was trapped.

'We'll have to hobble you, like the horses,' he said.

He drew her into his room. His books were put away in innumerable packing-cases and his jars and instruments were packed in grass in several large baskets but the eternal saucepan still bubbled on the brazier and four candles were alight on the altar. Chained to the staple in the wall, the child slept with only a torn blanket between his bare, narrow sides and the stone-flagged floor. Fresh weals of a beating marked his back.

'He's promising to be a good boy,' said Donally in a brooding voice. 'So he can sleep indoors, tonight, for we'll all be on the road tomorrow.'

How cool, sweet and pastel-tinted were the voices of the Professors; while the voices that grated daily on her nerves were edged with steel and ungrammatical. His voice was so gentle and familiar she was almost inclined to trust him until she saw the bloody chain with which he had beaten his son lying on the floor. He had been repairing his lurid cloak and the feathered garment was spread across the altar and shimmered in the candlelight. He offered her a drink from a leather flask. She refused.

'You'll excuse me if I continue my work. There won't be time for it, during the travelling.'

He put the flask down beside him and seated himself cross-legged on the altar; he began to ply his needle in the many coloured feathers.

She wondered if he would swoop down on wings to catch her if she made a dash for the door. He inquired in intimate tones:

'Does he misuse you?'

'How do you mean?' she asked carefully.

He batted his eyelids. His plucked brows were like sideways parentheses.

'Vile practices and unspeakable things, for instance,' he hedged.

'Such as what?' she asked, this time rudely.

'Fellatio and so on.'

'Would you consider that misuse?'

He opened his eyes wide as if surprised at her naïvety.

'Oh, yes, indeed; a vile practice and only to be discreetly mentioned in a language safely dead. The Romans were here and gone, of course, and, after them, Uther, when there were also wolves in the forests and even a lion or two if one can sort out fact from fiction, always a difficult task. And the milk-white unicorn, a heavily symbolic and extravagantly horned beast who could only be captured by a young virgin, which always proved the worst for it. Poor Jewel, in the same plight; though not, of course, milk white. It is going backwards, time is going backwards and coiling up; who let the spring go, I wonder, so that history wound back on itself?'

The melancholy whimsy of Professors gathered together over their after-dinner, home-brewed blackberry brandy when they would discuss apocalypses, utopias and so on. Marianne suppressed a yawn but, all the same, she felt at home. She went closer to the altar and watched the giant tailor repair his skin.

'God died, of course. Quite early. Do you think we should resurrect him, do you think we need him in this hypothetical landscape of ruin and forest in which we might or might not exist?'

'Do you desire the role yourself?'

'I prefer to remain anonymous, I'd rather choose to be the holy spirit. But I've often thought of grooming Jewel for some kind of mythopoeic role. If he never made the final rung of full-scale divinity, I'm sure he could easily acquire the kind of semi-legendary status that King Arthur had.' He began to laugh. 'He could be the Messiah of the Yahoos.'

He laughed so much he almost knocked over his bottle; he caught it just in time, drank again and again offered it to her.

'Come on, young lady. You might as well learn oblivion from their odious aqua vita now as later.'

'I don't plan to stay long enough.'

'What, you'd leave your husband to the melancholy pleasures of auto-fellatio? If you stay, I'll teach you necromancy.'

He was exceedingly drunk, no doubt passing most of the hours of darkness consuming their crude spirit to ease the pain. When she realized this, Marianne felt a certain exhilaration. Fallacious clouds of unreason rose from the saucepan in a green steam which also seemed to contain hallucinogenic properties since the skeleton in the recess occasionally twitched as if rattling his bones and the waxen Mary behind the altar swelled and diminished by fits and starts. But she could deduce methodologically that the Doctor's real though parti-coloured beard was dark at the roots on the red side and thus needed a fresh application of dye.

'Necromancy doesn't work,' she said.

'Nobody need ever know,' he whispered cunningly.

'Why did you run away from the Professors? Did they turn you out for doing something disgusting?'

'Oh, no,' he said. 'I came of my own free will.'

'Give me another aphorism, I feel the need for comfort.'

He thought for a while; then he said: 'The world becomes a dream and the dream, a world.'

'I hardly ever dream at all,' she said sadly. 'Jewel was angry with me when I told him, as if I was cheating.'

'I am trying to invent him as I go along but I am experiencing certain difficulties,' complained Donally. 'He won't keep still long enough. Creation from the void is more difficult than it would seem.'

Marianne saw the door open soundlessly. Jewel put his fingers to his lips to show her to keep quiet; he was carrying a knife between his teeth in order to have both his hands free. She was so angry he had followed her that she said at once: 'You've another visitor, give him some brandy.'

Jewel took away the knife and spat.

'And I'd meant to stab him, too,' he said with faint regret. He was hastily dressed and bare-footed but had taken the time to sling a mass of amulets around his neck. He shut the door behind him and lurked in the doorway with a beautiful, treacherous smile on his face.

'Venturing on to the stair for the purposes of nature, Jewel Lee Bradley, who should I find but your child bride intent on fleeing your embraces.'

'Not so much my embraces as fear of their consequences.'

'There's nowhere to go, dear,' said the Doctor. 'If there was, I would have found it.'

He held out the flask to Jewel who approached crabwise and accepted it. He sniffed it suspiciously, wiped the top and drank. A cold wind disturbed the rushes on the floor. Jewel's brown throat rippled and, watching him, Marianne wondered if the urge she felt to touch him was a need or a desire or if, contrary to what Donally said, both were functionally the same. The Doctor was perhaps experiencing a similar emotion. His hand came to rest on Jewel's shoulder. Marianne saw his fingernails were carefully, even beautifully, polished and manicured.

'Hands off,' said Jewel, shaking himself. 'I've told you often enough.'

'Show me my picture,' said Donally. 'Take off your shirt.'

He felt under the collar and began to pull off the garment; Jewel shrugged and allowed himself to be stripped.

'Kneel down.'

'You silly old man,' said Jewel almost tenderly and knelt. He parted his river of hair, exposing his neck as for the executioner's blade, and revealed again the monstrous tattoo, the Garden of Eden, the tree, the snake, the man, the woman and the apple.

'Observe the last work of art in the history of the world,' said Donally to Marianne. 'Observe the grace of line and the purity of execution.'

'You always did fancy me, you old bugger,' said Jewel, flinching a little as his tutor's hands slid lovingly over the incised marks.

'Not at all,' said Donally. 'Though how attractive you were at fifteen years old, wild as Cambyses and gentle as Ahasuerus.'

'I saw him for myself when he was fifteen,' said Marianne coldly. 'And I thought he looked a perfect savage.'

At that, Jewel raised his shaggy head and cast her a look of such naked distress that all at once she felt wounded herself; she gasped.

'It's a small world,' said Donally, satisfied with looking. He dropped the shirt back on Jewel's shoulders and tipped his bottle. 'It's as small a world as the Romans found and much smaller than Uther's, getting smaller all the time. Contracting, tightening, diminishing, shrinking.'

'Shall I offer her a real choice?' suggested Jewel. 'The more choices one has, the larger the world grows.'

'She's got no surprises for me, I assure you. I know which way her wind blows.'

But Jewel took up the candle, extended his hand to the young girl and said: 'Come.'

Donally sank back on the altar, banked by many sparkling feathers, his bottle in his hand, and watched them go with an air of applause. Outside the door, Jewel thrust the candle and the knife into her hand.

'Light your way out and defend yourself; feel free to go, get going.'

The flame cast a ring of pure light which illuminated only their faces so they were forced to look at each other closely. The terrible stench from the hall caught at Marianne's throat and somewhere a baby began to cry; she was filled with foreboding that her own children might one day weep in some hut or ruin among such wretchedness but she could no longer set her foot outside the compulsive circle, not, at least, tonight, desire it as much as she might. She made a convulsive movement as if in a last self-thwarted attempt to escape his magnetic field but his candle seemed the only light in the shrunken, darkened world. Yet she was determined to keep face, even if the world contracted a little more because she refused to take advantage of his offer.

'I'm tired, now,' she hedged. 'Besides, it's raining.'

He rearranged his face into an indecipherable smile. At his back stood Adam and Eve.

'How much . . . how much did it hurt when he tattooed you?'

'Nothing hurt me so much before or since. Why do you have such a morbid interest?'

'It is like the mark of Cain.'

'It was your brother I killed, not my own,' he said and pettishly snuffed out the candle flame with his fingers so they were in the dark again. At that, the wind began to howl dreadfully and Donally to savage the organ with his drunken fingers. Discordant chords zigzagged about the landing like bats. Marianne thought: 'He will wake the whole house up' and then realized the house was already stirring and waking. Points of light appeared at the mouths of rooms and footsteps began to patter, scarcely distinguishable from the sound of rain, for it was by now the moist beginnings of a new day. When they reached Jewel's tower, they found Mrs Green had been there before them and packed away the pots of paint, the jewellery, the weapons, the furs and the mattress into his wooden box, leaving only a rifle, some knives and his immediate clothing. He loaded the rifle in the opaline dawn, which almost entirely surrounded them for the wind and rain had brought the rest of the roof down and the room was now in the open air. The floor was an inch or so deep in rainwater; now the room belonged only to whatever birds might choose to nest in the walls next spring, to the rustling tree and to the devouring elements. A bird plopped on to the holly tree and shook its marbled feathers. It was a magpie.

'One for sorrow, two for joy, three for a girl, four for a boy,' said Jewel. He seemed to take a wry pleasure in this scrap of folklore.

'Where are we going?'

'The sea. Down south. For the winter, it's warmer. And we trade furs for fish and so on.'

In the meadow, the cavalcade was once again forming. The horses whinnied and stamped and the carts creaked, piled high with chattels. A cow lowed and an escaped goat ran frisking down towards the river, followed by a horde of screeching children. In their minds, the tribe was already up and away; the mansion echoed with the sounds of imminent departure and seemed quite hollow, once more abandoned. The kitchen was full of men snatching breakfast standing up; their already wet clothes steamed in the heat of Mrs Green's last cooking fire. Surrounded by incomprehensible business, Marianne detached herself; she found some bread and meat and took her accustomed place by the fire.

'You go in the cart with Mrs Green, like a bloody lady.'

'I'll go wherever you go.'

An expression of terror briefly crossed his face; she could not fail to recognize it, printed as it was on her memory.

'Oh, no, you won't, you'll do as I say.'

'Oh, no, I won't, I'll do as I want.'

He scowled and vanished into the throng. Gradually the room emptied but Marianne remained on her broken chair. Her eyes kept closing and at last she fell asleep, for she had not slept at all the previous night. In the bustle, she was left oblivious and when she woke abruptly, some time later, the kitchen was quite empty. Even the joints of meat were gone from the hooks in the ceiling. A child had deserted a crude wooden doll, which lay face down on the floor and the door swung on its hinges, creaking faintly, and that was all. In all the huge pile of rotting masonry nothing was left alive but the last embers in the hearth and they were dying. Marianne was stiff and cramped; she stretched and went to the door, momentarily hoping they had ridden off without her, but a black horse and a dappled pony stood together, ready saddled, in the yard, nosing for grass between the flagstones, so Jewel had evidently accepted her presence beside him as inevitable, with however many curses. The half-witted boy's plate lay turned over on its face. Marianne went back into the house, looking for Jewel. On the outside wall of the chapel, Donally had penned a last slogan, in case the wind blew anyone after them into the house and they might be able to read. The letters were slurred and staggered dreadfully but Marianne was able to make out the following: I THINK, THEREFORE I EXIST; BUT IF I TAKE TIME OFF FROM THINKING, WHAT THEN? She despised him for resorting to rhetorical questions. Jewel appeared in the doorway of the chapel, carrying a burning branch.

'They're all off on the road,' he said. 'I have stayed behind to burn the house down.'

She followed him along the aisle. She approved his decision.

'Will it burn in all this rain?'

'Rain's easing off.'

He pitched the brand at the organ, which was made of old, dry wood. In a few moments, the gilded cherubim were blazing cheerfully. Jewel and Marianne, united in a joint purpose, retreated to the doorway and watched the chapel consume itself; when the hides over the windows began to smoulder and the wax effigy spilled down its own front, they left the fire to proceed by itself and went to the hall. Just inside the front door, she found Jewel had already constructed a spiky pile of dead wood. He produced a fuse of fire by means of a tinder box which interested

Marianne very much for she had never seen one in use before. They
waited to make sure the flame had taken and then walked round the
house, along the terrace, past the backs of the disinterested statues.

They built another large bonfire in the kitchen on top of and around
the central table; on this, they emptied the contents of the hearth. She
had never seen the kitchen so well lit before; she noticed the ceiling was
totally covered by a grey canopy of cobwebs. Flames leaped from shelf
to shelf of the dresser. They went out into the yard, mounted their
horses, who were now beginning to be agitated by the flames and smoke
issuing from the kitchen door, and rode through the empty meadow,
across the river and up the bank, towards the woods. It was a clear, grey
morning and the rain came only in intermittent gusts but the wind blew
Jewel's hair like innumerable black flags. At the crest of the bank, they
halted and turned.

She saw the valley was now quite deserted, sunk in dreary autumn,
for it was growing late in the year. The silence of the dripping woods
oppressed her. She buried her hands in the pony's mane. The Barbarians
had come and gone and left only the dung heap already dissolving in
the rain, a few shards of broken pottery, a grave marked with the skull
of a horse and a forlornly flapping shirt, left out to dry on a bush and
forgotten; but Jewel intended nothing should remain. For a moment,
the shipwrecked building glowed with interior incandescence; then there
was a tremendous roaring crash and the roof caved in, releasing a
spiralling jet of flame so tall it licked the lowest clouds and turned the
sky pink.

Within the twinkling of an eye, the eclectic façade was consumed
and the internal structure of the house revealed, ablaze, caging an
intense white core which radiated red, yellow and mauve flames. The
line of blackened statues stretched their arms forth, as if attempting to
flee the fire which nevertheless engulfed them. The river flared with
reflections of the tumultuous inferno and terrified birds started upwards
from surrounding trees. Jewel's horse showed the whites of its eyes and
reared; he muttered some words to it and, dancing sideways, it quieted.
The wind blew sparks into their faces. Then an inner floor gave with a
rending roar and it was as though a fiery and all-devouring lion pounced
upon the meadow. The terrace itself vanished. The dead rose trees

blazed. Distant thunder rumbled behind the sky. The grass charred and leaves shrivelled up and dropped from the trees. The wind tossed tides of blazing debris hither and thither around the valley.

'And will the whole forest catch fire?' she asked.

'Maybe,' he said with a certain anticipatory relish. His eyes were discs of reflected flame. He turned his horse into the wood, gesturing her to follow, and soon they reached a green road, leaving behind them a valley occupied by fire alone. A pheasant rattled upwards from the grass at their approach. Then they caught up with the last lagging travellers and were absorbed into a group again.

The travelling required a great deal of organization. She saw the Bradleys had a certain dislike of delegating authority; even Precious, though he was only fifteen, would give orders to men two or three times his own age and have them obeyed. The brothers preferred to take upon themselves the task of combing the woods at the side of the road for concealed attackers or spying out the road ahead in case a Professor convoy was seen approaching. Movement itself progressed so slowly that distance, like time, no longer had a practical application; motion became another aspect of the road. Now the travellers were in their element, a steady, persevering progression from nowhere to nowhere, in featureless, colourless weather. Sometimes they stopped, to rest the horses or to eat. A blackbird with one startling white wing came hopping for crumbs.

'Scavengers,' remarked Jewel. 'What will the birds do when we're gone?'

Mrs Green pulled his sleeve and drew him a little to one side. Two or three of the brothers had gathered around them, to get some food.

'Jewel, my duck, another baby is sick, Annie's baby, and the travelling is harming it. She didn't say nothing, not this morning.'

'No,' said Jewel. 'She wouldn't have wanted to be left behind.'

'Would you have left a woman and a child behind because the child was sick?' exclaimed Marianne.

'That would depend on the disease,' he replied. 'But we always abandon the most cruelly deformed of the new born in the forest. What else did you expect?'

He sank into silence, tearing up blades of wet grass. Johnny lay down carelessly at rest beside his brother; he turned his face up to the cool sun, just now appearing from behind a cloud, and whistled a snatch of tune. Jewel struck him on the mouth with a hand heavy with rings. Johnny's lip cut and trickled blood. Johnny knocked Jewel down. The brothers fought in the long grass, clawing and punching one another until Johnny knelt on his half-brother's belly methodically hitting Jewel's face again and again. The fight began so unexpectedly and reached its climax so swiftly Marianne was transfixed but Mrs Green took a pail of water which stood ready for drinking and calmly emptied it over them both, as Marianne had seen Worker women pour water on cats battling under domestic moons. Johnny dashed the water from his eyes, swearing, and scrambled off Jewel, who stretched out and pressed his face into the ground.

'Brothers should be friends,' said Mrs Green sententiously. 'You go and change your wet clothes and let Jewel alone.'

'He started it,' said Johnny truculently, wringing water from his braided hair.

'Be that as it may, you should show respect for him, not scrap with him like kids.'

Around them, children, rested and fed, began to play a small game, running about in a flush of refreshed spirits. Donally's son, for a wonder released from his chain, wandered up to them and looked curiously at Jewel flat on the ground.

'What's the matter with him?' he asked Mrs Green.

Jewel caught the boy's ankle with one hand and overturned him so he sprawled and began to bellow.

'He's cussed,' said Johnny, removing his soaked shirt to reveal a marvellous, lithe, muscular torso decorated with a bird in blue and red. He went off to find himself some fresh clothing. Jewel propped himself on one elbow and watched the half-witted boy do his weeping for him. Then he took a ring with a red stone off his third finger and offered it to the boy on the palm of his hand.

'For me?' demanded the half-wit, stopping crying at once.

'Why not? Don't eat it, mind.'

'You must think I'm pretty stupid,' said the boy. He held the ring to the light and the stone flashed the deepest red. He put it on his finger and admired his hand. Then lost interest.

'Can I have some bread as well?'

'Give him some bread.' The right side of Jewel's face was already beginning to discolour. The boy received a crust and scampered off. Jewel turned back to his foster-mother.

'What's wrong with Annie's baby?'

She shrugged and did not reply except to make the sign against the evil eye which Marianne had never seen her do before. Then the journey continued. In the middle of the afternoon, Marianne arrived at the top of a hill and found she could see for miles across a melancholy terrain of deep gulfs, pools, abysses, pits, quagmires, dikes and fens divided by long stretches of thick woodland. They had reached a region where the hedgerows were composed solely of those plants with cutting leaves whose fruits were globes of poison. The riders cuffed the heads of their inquisitive mounts away from the sides of the road but the plants grew in the roadway, also, and cruelly cut open bare feet and also the legs and underparts of the horses. And once more it began to rain. She wondered whether the horses would one day become amphibious if they continued to spend so much time in the wet.

They camped in a discarded village. Mrs Green had a cottage with enough roof left to keep out the rain and she smuggled Annie and the sick baby in with her, so it would be sheltered and warm and the Doctor would not see it and order it out. The cottage had two rooms, one of them with a useable fireplace, once the birds' nests had been cleared from the chimney. There were two human skeletons in the wreckage of a bed in the other room. The sheets had rotted away. The brothers removed all this without speaking. They chopped what remained of the furniture for firewood but left the rags at the broken windows.

'You sleep by the fire with Mrs Green and Annie,' said Jewel to Marianne. Annie was the first Barbarian woman she had encountered, Jewel's cousin they met gathering mushrooms. She held her six months' baby in her arms and stared dumbly at Marianne as if Marianne were to blame. The baby's father had died of tetanus the previous spring; now she had only her baby.

'I'll sleep with you,' Marianne affirmed obstinately.

Mrs Green cooked a meagre stew. After they had eaten, the other five men vanished to play the game with bones and to drink in another cottage but Jewel stayed with the women, squatting on his haunches beside the fire, for there was still ill-feeling between him and Johnny. From time to time, he coughed. The stone-flagged floor had a thick, soft carpet of dust, criss-crossed in herring-bone patterns by the feet of mice. Mrs Green put the cooking pots and the dishes from which they had eaten out to wash clean in the rain. Annie sat on the edge of a mattress and cradled her baby in a blanket in her arms.

'Pity the poor folks out in the cold tonight without a roof over their heads,' said Mrs Green comfortably.

Jewel spread his fingers over his bruised face and said nothing. Mrs Green sat beside Annie and took her hand. Marianne knelt beside the fire; rain tumbled down the chimney and buzzed upon the flames. A perfect stillness descended upon them. They all sat so perfectly without movement it was as if the night supported itself upon the pillars of their stillness and nobody dared move. This stillness at last began to affect Marianne curiously; she had a great desire to laugh. Instead, she spoke quite softly, so as to disturb nothing.

'Give me your comb,' she said to Jewel. 'I'll comb your hair for you.'

He lowered his hand and revealed red eyes surprised and wary but soon she held him on her lap, combing out his hair in a prolonged, artificial caress. The eyes of the other two women followed the strokes of her hand as if mesmerized. And Marianne knew in her heart that none of this was real; that it was a kind of enchantment. She was in no-man's-land. She watched her arm rise and fall, so newly gaudy a sleeve, and saw no shadow imaging the movements of her arm, so she knew herself to be dreaming and was all at once immensely relieved, so relieved she allowed herself a small ripple of unforgivable laughter. At that, the pillars collapsed and night tumbled into the room. The baby shrieked like an uprooted mandrake. Annie began to shriek, also. A stream of incoherent cries gushed from her mouth and Jewel took the comb from Marianne's hand and sat upright.

'She says you're laughing at her,' he interpreted. 'She says you're killing her baby by laughing at her. What are you going to do about it?'

Marianne stared unbelievingly at the woman who had lost all restraint and foamed and moaned upon the mattress whether she was real or not.

'I don't know,' she said. 'I don't know at all. Tell me what to do.'

'Kiss her,' said Jewel and spat into the fire.

'She hates me.'

'Kiss her. Show her you're made of flesh and blood.'

'What do you mean, do you mean show her pity?'

'Fuck off,' he said and winced.

He pierced her with the sharp, hard, assessing gaze she had seen on his face the morning after they were married. She realized that all were now regarding her with this same, torturing, adamantine intensity and she stood up, perplexed and irritated. The baby's screams modulated to a dull moaning.

Marianne reached out uncertainly, for she did not know how to approach a woman worn to such strange shapes by hardship and fear. Also, she thought Annie might have a knife in the waistband of her skirt and stab her when she came near enough. Then she thought she might catch an infection off the baby and die herself. Besides, she did not want to admit the unknown woman's suffering was real. She resented her husband passionately since he had invented another intolerable ordeal for her apparently on the spur of the moment. She turned to run into the other room, away from them all.

'Kiss her,' said Jewel for the third time, with such an undertone of menace she knew there was nothing for it. She started a slow walk as if to the scaffold, one foot before the other, running a gauntlet of eyes like blades. Annie drew one hand from the folds of her shawl and made the magic, protective sign.

'Don't do that,' said Jewel and Annie stopped as if she were exactly his creature and would do anything he said. Her hand was crooked in mid-air and Marianne pressed her dry lips against it. She kissed the woman's hand but knew that was not enough so she kissed her forehead and looked at Jewel to see if she should kiss her mouth. Jewel gave no indication as to what either of them should do now. Annie shrank away but she was as much afraid of Jewel's displeasure as she was of Marianne and he had perversely ceased to give her signals. Marianne saw the baby's bleared, red face pressed against a breast from which it was too ill to suck and helplessly she began to cry. Her tears splashed on Annie's cheek. Annie touched them with her finger and then licked her finger to see if they were salt enough. Marianne slid down to her knees, sobbing as if her heart was breaking. Annie pushed the girl away and turned her back on her with a sigh.

'I'm sure she's got nothing against you, really, Marianne, dear,' said Mrs Green.

Marianne pressed her fists into her eyes but tears ran through the spaces between her knuckles.

'Put her to bed,' said Mrs Green.

Jewel lifted her up by the shoulders and transferred her to the other room. She was crying so much she could not see where she was going. He dumped her on the heap of blankets, and left her there while the rain dripped all around her, until she cried herself to sleep. She did not wake up when he came to bed himself but she woke much later, in the middle of the night, when Mrs Green came shaking him, for in sleep they had unconsciously tangled together for warmth and it was impossible for one to wake without the other.

'Come and dig the grave,' said Mrs Green without preliminaries. She shielded the flame of a little lamp with her hand so as not to wake the other brothers who now snored about them.

'Burn him,' said Jewel.

'I refuse to burn a child on a domestic fire,' said Mrs Green.

'You are a woman of many refinements,' said Jewel sombrely.

He rolled on to the floor. Still the rain came down.

'Come on, Marianne, come see me at my work.'

Rainwater pooled on the rotten floorboards and, outside, the hoof-churned earth had turned to knee-high, liquid mud. Mrs Green silently handed Jewel a spade. Both their faces seemed made of seamed rock. The woman stood in the doorway. Annie held her child, which was wrapped in a clean pillowslip as there was no time to improvise a coffin. Enough of the firelight shone through the open door for Jewel to see what he was doing. No other lights showed in the houses and there was neither moon nor stars, only rain. Jewel's white shirt grew dark with mud and Marianne could hardly see the outline of his body, though she could hear the succulent noise of the spade. Now and then it clinked on a stone.

'Dig deep enough so the dogs won't find him before morning,' warned Mrs Green.

'Ah, grant me some competence,' he replied.

At last he said: 'Deep enough.'

Annie ducked into the rain and handed the heavy pillowslip to him.

'He's only a little bit of a thing to go by hisself,' she said in wonder. She crouched down in the mud at the edge of the hole and patted down the earth on top of him tenderly, as if making sure the baby was covered up well enough. They returned to the cottage soaked to the skin and plastered with mud. Mrs Green had taken in the black pot and boiled the water it contained: she washed Annie's face and hands, took off her dirty clothes and persuaded her to lie down, rocking her in her arms till she slept. Jewel washed silently. Marianne could not cry any more; she sat propped vacantly against the wall.

'It's almost morning,' he said and, kneeling before the fire, bent forward to dry his tangled hair, hiding a face which Marianne's swollen eyes saw for one moment entirely blasted of life and pared to the appalling integrity of bare bone.

6

Where the ground was naturally moist were brakes of sedges, flags and rushes but, elsewhere, the road was fringed with thorn bushes hung with grey, green and russet lichen. In those places where a spring had forced its way through the concrete, the roadway flowed like a river. Sometimes a fall of earth or rock almost obliterated the way and often the boughs of forest trees locked over their heads so the road echoed like a whispering gallery. Some warmish, moist days succeeded the rain and the travellers were tormented by mosquitoes but, after that, a dry day proved worst of all for the mud turned to white dust which choked them and caked their eyes and nostrils while flies and gnats danced in poisonous attendance.

'You need some cool, grey days for the travelling, ideally,' said Mrs Green.

At night, they slept beneath skin tents or inside whatever buildings they found which could afford a little protection. Nothing was permanent nor was any one night in any way as the previous night had been; the day was absolutely devoted to perpetual motion and Marianne felt herself stretched out upon the road as if it were a rack. Boredom and exhaustion conspired to erode her formerly complacent idea of herself. She could find no logic to account for her presence nor for that of the people around her nor any familiar, sequential logic at all in this shifting world; for that consciousness of reason in which her own had ripened was now withering away and she might soon be prepared to accept, since it was coherent, whatever malign structure of the world with which the shaman who rode the donkey should one day choose to present her. She often thought of the baby who had been planted in the ground like a bitter seed which would not germinate but she could make no sense of it and often wondered why she had cried so much that night.

Though the rest of the tribe had long since abandoned this pursuit, the Doctor continued to watch her. The cracked mirrors of his dark glasses revealed all manner of potentialities for Marianne, modes of being to which she might aspire just as soon as she threw away her reason as of no further use to her, since it scarcely helped her to construe the enigmas all about her. Whether in his black furs or his dark suit, Donally remained obscenely spry. His parti-coloured beard sang out two confident notes of artificial colour all day and, in the evenings, she could hear him play geometric melodies upon a flute, as he sat underneath a tree. She imaged his snake extending a no less colourful head than his own from the beribboned bars of its cage, to listen to the music; maybe even the blurred plastic flowers which clung to the bars would open again fresh perfumed petals at the powerful beauty of the sound. For he was an excellent musician.

The roads were arteries which no longer sprang from a heart. Once the cities were gone, the roads reverted to an older function; they were used for the most existential kind of travelling, that nomadic peregrination which is an end in itself, and the Barbarians preferred to avoid the cities altogether, or, if this proved impossible, to go through the outskirts by day. This distaste for the ruins did not spring from superstition since parties of armed horsemen often made forays into their depths, seeking what they could find; but the Out People had taken to the cities, living there in holes in the ground.

'But I used to go for endless rambles in the ruins beside my home and never saw anyone,' she said to Jewel.

'They must have thought you were an angel and fled you from fear. They think the Professor villages are the earthly paradise and full of terrible angels with fiery swords to keep them out.'

But they did not fear the Barbarians and the cavalcade of wagons was difficult to defend from attack, as Marianne was to discover.

She was on foot, to spare the horses. She had chosen to walk near the front of the line, that day, away from Mrs Green and her old saws. The brothers took it in shifts to search the surroundings for enemies of various kinds and, when Jewel's shift was over, he came and walked beside Marianne, perhaps to keep an eye on her. When she glanced at him, he looked as insubstantial as if cut from paper. From time to time, he coughed. They entered the margins of the ruins towards the end of a lowering, windless morning.

To the left, the ground fell away in rust-stained, thorny swampland; to the right, there rose above them a wall of scarified concrete pierced with holes through which could be seen a leathern sky that seemed to exude sweat. This wall marked the boundary of a cratered expanse of fallen towers like a mouthful of rotten teeth and a whirlpool of crows drearily circled above it, filling the humid air with their melancholy cawing. The light that morning was yellow and garish. Random patches of fog now and then obscured the view and hung motionless in many places above the swamp. The road was bad. The original surface had deeply cracked into huge, irregular segments and the jagged interstices stuck up into the air. In these crevices, such plants as love arid places sprouted amidst pebbles, bones and skulls. The carts rolled drunkenly and often baggage would spill from them, scattering all manner of household implements everywhere. A coop of chickens fell, broke open and emitted a squawking flock immediately pursued with cheerful cries which died away lifelessly for the place was ominous.

Marianne stared at the back of the woman in front of her, who led a skinny cow by the bridle. She did not know this woman's name but soon she knew her back by heart. It was the back of a long skirt made of a dark grey blanket, and of a shirt embroidered with five pointed stars, the soles of two bare feet shod with horn which she only saw one at a time, and the back of a sleeveless coat of fringed leather down which hung two brown plaits trimmed with rags. And then she saw an arrow stuck and quivering in this back, in the middle of the leather jacket, between the plaits, an arrow tipped with red come out of the blue, from nowhere.

Everything changed immediately. The woman grunted and fell forward on her face. Her terrified cow took to its heels and foundered miserably in the bog. Jewel seized Marianne and, flinging her sideways from the road, half dragged and half carried her across the slithering ground as fresh arrows fell around them until he pushed her down behind a piece of wall, beside a clump of thorns, in a position of precarious safety.

She fell on her face in the mud and could see nothing but heard a burst of gunfire, a clatter of hooves, a crash as of falling masonry and some wailing. She guessed Jewel was firing a rifle but he was lying above her and she realized with some bewilderment he was protecting her with his body. She heard some quick and whizzing sounds – the air, parted by arrows. Yet all this happened so quickly her mind's eye still held the single image, the shaft of the arrow in the leather jacket, the arrow quivering. Then she found herself battered by movement but half released, half still pressed against the wall; he seemed to be fighting with someone. She struggled away from the twining bodies and crouched under the thorn bush, wiping her eyes.

Yellowish fog had descended and cut them off entirely so she, Jewel and the thing with which he fought were all contained within a sight-less and opaque bubble of air. It was the fourth time she had seen Jewel fighting and the third time she had seen him fighting for his life. His attacker this time was naked, but for a loincloth of animal skin, and covered with festering sores. His arms were very short because they lacked elbows and were unnaturally hinged too low down on a body curiously warped and out of true. His face was marked with a gigantic cicatrice and the nose had been omitted; his nostrils were twin pits between his eyes. His canine teeth had grown into fangs. He was armed with a knife. They splashed and sprawled in the mud until Jewel managed to knock this knife from the other's hand; then Jewel began to cough and could fight no more, choking as he was in the grasp of a less tangible enemy.

The warped man caught Jewel's abundant hair, pulled back his head and was about to bite him in the throat when Marianne stabbed him in the small of the back, in the region of the kidneys, with his own knife. He gurgled, oozed excrement and jerked back and forth. She stabbed him several times more, surprised to see how quickly the blood gushed out. Beneath this death agony, Jewel now lay helpless and Marianne blindly continued to hack away until the creature was no more than a piece of abused flesh which did not continue to move.

Jewel opened his eyes. A little blood dribbled from the corner of his own mouth. The obscene head lay on his shoulder. At length he gestured to Marianne to remove the corpse and, dropping her reeking blade, she did so. He got to his knees and examined the wounds she had made.

'I'll have to learn you to shoot,' he said. 'You haven't half messed him up, haven't you, you, you haven't half butchered him.'

While they wallowed in the mud, the fog became suffused with light. Jewel laid the corpse on its back, took two rings from his fingers, closed the eyes and weighed the eyelids down. Marianne leaned against the broken wall, panting for breath. They were both thickly caked with various kinds of filth. The fog became quite white and blew away completely. Twenty yards or so away from them, they saw the road. The wall where the Out People had ambushed them was pocked with bullet holes and the Doctor prowled up and down among the slain, chanting prayers, for the fighting was over.

Those killed lay in undignified heaps. Amongst the Out People, the human form acquired fantastic shapes. One man had furled ears as pale, delicate and extensive as Arum lilies. Another was scaled all over, with webbed hands and feet. Few had the conventional complement of limbs or features and most bore marks of nameless diseases. Some were ludicrously attenuated, with arms and legs twice as long as those of natural men, but one was perfect in all things but a perfect miniature, scarcely two feet long from tip to tip.

'There you are,' said Jewel to his tutor. 'The phenomenon of man.'

'I don't believe they're men at all,' said Marianne, who had killed the warped man out of blind repugnance only to obliterate what seemed to her a cruel parody of life.

'Necessity suggests we adopt a standard pattern,' said Donally. 'We abhor variations, though it may be a short-sighted measure, at that, if we are to adapt to survive. Perhaps we should seriously reconsider as to whether form makes the man.'

Jewel thought for a while.

'Those who live in marshes ought to grow web feet,' he suggested and laughed so much the bereaved were startled.

The greater part of the cavalcade had escaped the attack, which had focused unwisely on the front of the line, and the Out People had been easily routed for they were by no means cunning. Their sinister arrows killed only the one woman, a child and an old man, though several others had been wounded and now stoically awaited blood poisoning. While the bodies were being disposed of, the carts went forward to leave this dangerous place as soon as possible and men with guns crouched along the wall, to cover them.

Jewel, Blue, Bendigo and Jacob were all digging graves beside the road, a communal hole for the Out People but one each for the members of the tribe. Donally stood beside them, riffling through the Book of Common Prayer, and Marianne waited beside her husband, combing the dry mud out of her hair with her fingers. She felt neither shame nor horror, only a release from boredom and, with it, a certain sense of well-being. Since she had saved Jewel's life again, she wondered whether it was indeed hers to dispose of in entirety. A rifle cracked and soon they tossed into the hole a being of indeterminate sex equipped with breasts, testicles and a light but total covering of chestnut fur. Then a horseman leaped from the ruins dragging a prisoner on the end of the rope, a prisoner who bounced and rebounded from the road like a stuffed skin but wept. It was Precious, all trussed up with ropes but for his feet.

'Precious was supposed to search the wall,' said Johnny. 'That was his duty. Who can you trust if not your kin?'

'Three people died,' said Jewel wearily to Precious. 'What have you to say to that?'

Precious was so frightened he could hardly stand upright.

'I found some honey in a tree,' he said. 'I was eating honey.'

'Honey,' repeated Jewel. Their foster-mother lifted her skirts fastidiously out of the dirt and picked her way towards them.

'He was eating honey and let the Out People through,' said Jewel sullenly, gesturing towards Precious.

'He's only a kid,' said Mrs Green. 'He's fifteen years old.'

'Power is forced to display persuasive force,' said Donally, folding his hands into his sleeves. Marianne saw his words as if in red paint written on the shattered wall.

'You deserve to be hung,' said Jewel to his brother. 'But instead I shall have to whip you, as soon as I can find a tree to tie you to. And now you can dig.'

When this task was finished and Donally had performed a rite or two, they rode on. Mrs Green had Jewel's black horse while he walked beside her. She was obviously suffering some sort of conflict.

'It seems so hard,' she said. 'And he no more than a child.'

Nobody talked to Precious, who stumbled behind them, weeping.

'No thanks to Precious we're not all dead,' said Jewel, on whose face the mud had dried into a mask.

'Precious is half your own brother and some of your own flesh and blood.'

'All the more reason it's I who should whip him.'

As they reached the open country, they left the fog, the swamp and the lurid light behind them; an afternoon sun came out to shine and they came to a region of bracken covered downs. Precious was to be punished in the evening since then it would be most impressive. He lurched at Johnny's heels with his hands tied together behind his back and received nothing to eat or drink all the rest of the day. As evening approached, they arrived at some farm buildings. The corrugated iron roof of the barn was a cobweb of dark red rust, tenuous as the wing of a moth, and it was no longer possible to tell where the fields had been, but an orchard had shed so many apples into the long grass that a herd of wild pigs had settled there to gorge themselves and trampled the foliage flat.

The wild pigs were long, pale animals with flapping pink ears and eyes like redcurrants. Their snouts quivered as they scrambled over one another to escape the first bullets of the outriders and they squealed and grunted dreadfully. The beautiful light of early evening turned them to pigs of gold. Those who did not instantly become pork raced off over the downs with a surprising turn of speed. The village of tents went up and fires were started. Johnny lashed Precious by the wrists to the low bough of an apple tree and left him there, to wait. The tribe gradually assembled round the apple tree and an air of anticipation lent unusual animation to each weathered face.

The Doctor unpacked and donned his wooden mask and feather robe. This rainbow giant stood like a polychrome abstraction beside the prisoner, a horsewhip in his hand. And Jewel's face was clay; neither wore their proper faces for this occasion. Donally handed Jewel the whip and, taking off his shirt, Jewel went to the tree. Marianne saw the other apple tree, the one he carried with him, and this tattooed tree seemed to throb with life, as if it were the visible tree of the young man's blood, the tree which sustained him, and no decorative pattern at all; she found she was breathless.

'Justice,' he said.

The children all sat together to watch; Jen, Donally's son and the other ones sat hushed with expectation, the performance of justice might have been some long-promised treat. Annie watched with huge eyes and her mouth ajar; perhaps she would be comforted by the sight of Precious' pain or saw his punishment as a retribution on some more impersonal object. The boy had already been hanging by his hands for some time. His face was turned inwards to the leafless core of the tree. In a ritual fashion, with a stately gesture, Donally ripped off his shirt, also. His feet trailed upon the ground. He had been sentenced to twenty lashes. After the second stroke, Donally's son whimpered out loud, broke from the circle and ran away into the bracken.

After the fifth, a girl began to cry. At the eighth, Precious started to bleed profusely. Marianne could no longer bear to watch after the tenth stroke, when he was as striped as a bloody tiger and swung heavily under the blows like a carpet being beaten. The whip whirred and thumped; Precious grunted at its impact, all in all a mechanical repetition of sounds. She saw that Jewel had become mechanical.

He was nothing but the idea of that power which men fear to offend; his back flexed and his arm rose and fell. The snake on his back flicked its tongue in and out with the play of muscle beneath the skin and the tattooed Adam appeared to flinch again and again from the apple which Eve again and again leaned forward to offer him until it seemed that the moving picture of an endless temptation was projecting on Jewel's surfaces, an uncompleted series of actions with no conclusion, caught in a groove of time. And Jewel was also caught in this groove of time; frozen in the act of punishment, he was concealed within a mask which covered his entire body, a man no longer. Had they used to put hoods over hangmen in the old days in case they caught sight of themselves in mirrors and died of fright? When the strokes ceased, she looked again. Jewel dropped the whip and ran to the tree. He cut Precious down and caught him in his arms as he fell forward.

'It's not my fault,' said Jewel. 'I love you best.'

Either from pride or spite, Precious had not yet lost consciousness.

'Then whose fault is it, you bastard?' he said.

With his last remaining strength, he spat in Jewel's face, staggered

from his embrace and tumbled down in a faint. Jewel stood dazed and
vacant, running with sweat, while Mrs Green came with water and
cloths to attend to Precious. She conspicuously ignored her eldest, who
put his hand against the tree, to support himself, and then clutched the
trunk quite insanely, almost with desire; Marianne would have liked to
touch him but, on the other hand, he disgusted her. Murmuring, the
crowd dispersed for justice had been done upon the honey thief and
there was no more entertainment that night. Donally began to sort
through a basketful of green herbs and whistle a mathematical baroque
tune. The light was so thick and delicious looking it could have been
eaten with a spoon for the evening was as unnaturally warm and sweet
as fresh jam.

Unnoticed, Marianne wandered away through the barrier of carts
drawn up in a defensive circle. The horses grazed peacefully and did
not look up as she passed. Her shoes were so worn they were as good
as useless so she took them off and threw them away; the cool grass
curled round her feet like loving tongues as she wandered downhill,
through a tangle of weeds mixed with wild grains, until the encampment was only the marks of fires in the sky and she was alone. She found
a thicket of hazels and, beyond it, a stream choked with reeds.

She sat on the bank and paddled her hand in the standing water.
The setting sun beamed red darts through the brown stems of hazel
and dyed the still stream with henna. The hazels were covered with
nuts. She listened to the soft plop of water through her fingers. She
was moist with sweat and had scarcely taken off her clothes for weeks,
had slept, walked, ridden, attended a burial, killed a man/not-man and
gone to a public execution of justice in the same shirt and trousers; it
was a wonder she was not yet overwhelmed with lice, though she often
trapped a flea. She put her burning cheek flat down against the cool
face of the water and, when she raised her head, the half-witted boy
was squatting on the bank beside her, as if they had made a secret
assignation for this place but had forgotten to mention it to one another.
Some trick of the amber light turned his bare shoulders a healthier
colour than usual. He picked his nose with the finger that wore Jewel's
ruby ring, if it were a real ruby and not glass. She saw the mark of his
collar round his neck.

'Why does your father keep you chained up so much?' she asked him.

'He's afraid of me because I have better fits than he does,' said the boy. 'Watch me.'

He rolled his eyes, foamed at the mouth and threshed about on the grass so vigorously she was afraid he would hurt himself.

'Stop it,' she said firmly. He shuddered to a standstill and fixed her with white, astonished eyes. His foam-flecked tongue lolled over his pale, cracked, swollen lips.

'Of course, you're Jewel's woman, aren't you,' he said as though this explained everything.

'I'm his wife,' she said.

'Same thing.'

'No, it isn't. There's no choice in being a wife. It is entirely out of one's hands.'

He wagged his dirty brown head; he did not understand her.

'It's the same thing,' he insisted.

'No.'

''Tis.'

'No.'

''Tis! 'Tis! 'Tis!' Again he rolled over and over shouting ''Tis!' in a cracked, imperious voice until Marianne said firmly: 'You're making a fool of yourself.'

He started up, gazing at her with something like wonder because she stopped him.

'What do you mean?'

He was panting. The serpents on his breast writhed in and out and curled round the old bruises on his ribs. He raised his hands and hid behind them, squinting through his fingers at her; his movements were sinuous but erratic, if he had known how to be graceful it would have been delightful to watch him. He rocked back and forth on his heels until, without the shadow of a warning, he jumped on her. He was weightless as a hollow-boned bird or an insect that carries its structure on its outside without a cargo within. She could have pushed him away maybe with one finger, even have thrown him into the stream had she wished to defend herself but she realized this was the first opportunity she had had to betray her husband and instantly she took advantage of it.

The gaunt, crazy, shameless child rolled her among the roots for a while as he probed underneath her clothes with fingers amazingly long and delicate but, it would seem, moved more by curiosity than desire and she wondered if he were too young to do it so she unbuttoned her shirt and rubbed his wet mouth against her breasts for him. The tips of her breasts were so tender she whined under her breath and he became very excited. He began to mutter incomprehensible snatches of his father's prayers and maxims and she roughly seized hold of him and crushed him inside her with her hand for she had not sufficient patience to rely on instinct. He made two or three huge thrusts and came with such a terrible cry it seemed the loss of his virginity caused him as much anguish or, at least, consternation as the loss of her own had done. He slid weakly out of her, shivering, but she retained him in her arms and kissed the tangles of his hair. She was unsatisfied but full of pleasure because she had done something irreparable, though she was not yet quite sure what it was. So they lay there for a while in the inexpressible stillness and sombre colours of evening. He touched her without sensible contact for his frail body gave out no warmth.

'Did you know you're in the family way,' he said in a voice like a thread of glass.

She saw the ghost of a crescent moon floating in the coppery sky over a red down, between the hazel twigs. Donally's child was never to be believed even when he stubbornly insisted:

'Here, Jewel's put a kid up you.'

He licked the swollen nipple of her right breast softly and laughed to himself. He had another question.

'Does he do you often?'

'I've never seen his face, in bed with him; perhaps it was never him at all, perhaps something else.'

Because of this, it occurred to her to raise his head so she could scrutinize his own face. It was soft and formless, a fat, drooping mouth and the huge, lost eyes of a child in a wood menaced by the nightingale. Now the sun was down, he was as white as if it ordinarily forbore to touch him. There was a long scratch down his cheek. He shook himself free and lay down on top of her again. He ran his tongue along the downy groove between her breasts.

'Does he know?'

'Does he know what?'

'That you're going to have a baby.'

'How do you know, yourself?'

'I think you are,' he said. 'Am I your friend?'

A wind shifted the reeds and he shivered again. He quite forgot the question he had just asked her and remarked accusingly:

'I'm cold.'

She was caught in a storm of warmth of heart; she wanted to fold him into her, where it was warm and nobody could harm him, poor, lucid, mindless child of chaos now sucking her as if he expected to find milk. She stroked his scarred sides and thought: 'Is he right, am I pregnant? I might be, I never thought about it, not till the last night in the old house, I never bothered to watch for the signs.' These signs were cessation of menstruation; morning sickness; indigestion; constipation. She laughed, because all these things seemed so undignified and he raised those huge, wondering eyes of palest grey. She was suddenly unnerved for these eyes might not reflect a lack of mind at all but an intelligence which, though extreme, ran along a parallel course which did not abut on her own and, maybe, on nobody else's.

'Go away, now, and leave me alone.'

He nodded obediently and stood up.

'Here, you silly –'

She sat upright and fastened his ragged trousers for him. He curled his fingers in her short hair and sang a phrase from one of his father's tunes. As if answering him, a bird trilled out from a neighbouring tree; perhaps it was a nightingale for the Doctor's son stopped singing at once, aghast.

'But what name will you give it?'

'Give what?'

'Jewel's kid.'

'Modo or Mahu,' she improvised.

'You can't catch me,' he said. 'You're joking. You don't believe me, do you?'

In the perfect innocence of his lambent regard, she experienced utter conviction and, with it, a desolating sorrow. Half unconsciously, she drew her shirt over her breasts again in order to hide them from him.

'I do believe you,' she said.

He scratched an insect bite on his upper arm, gave her a slack smile which showed he had decided to become an idiot again and slipped away through the thicket like a pale fish. Marianne lay down on the grass, aching with sorrow. After a while, she took off her clothes and immersed herself in the stream. There was an unexpectedly strong tug of current; she half wanted to let it take her away with it, down to a river, down the wide river perhaps to arrive, drowned and dead, long before the tribe at the unknown sea. But instead she washed herself carefully again and again, sluicing the cold water between her thighs to wash away every trace of the boy's casual visitation until the light began to fade and the water turn black. She dried herself on her clothes and put them on again. They stuck to her wetly and she was chilled through, though the evening was still warm.

The brothers had eaten and now lounged around their private fire. Johnny was cleaning a rifle, as if trapped in a vignette of Barbarian life, and Precious was nowhere to be seen, probably sleeping in a tent. Mrs Green sat on an upturned bucket with the child Jen wedged between her knees, going through her hair with a fine comb. Jewel lay on his face and Marianne was all at once convinced he was dead and she had helped to kill him, that his heart had stopped at perhaps the precise moment when the boy had launched himself on to her belly. Jewel was a dead pile of rags, bone and hair and she flung herself down beside him in a state of the wildest confusion, for the idea that he was dead was all at once unbearable.

'Wherever have you been, dear?' asked Mrs Green, trapping a flea and crushing it between the nails of her forefinger and thumb. 'Hush up,' she admonished Jen, who was squealing to have her hair tugged so.

Marianne could make no answer because she was so sure Jewel was dead.

'She's been sending signals to the Professors,' suggested Johnny, briefly levelling the rifle at her and showing his teeth.

'She's been bewitching the horses,' said Bendigo. It was a perilous kind of joking. At any moment, they might turn against her.

'Don't go on at her, poor thing, she looks worn out.'

Jewel's hand of ravisher, murderer and grave-digger acquired a form of life and grasped her elbow. She could have wept with relief but found she had temporarily forgotten how to cry.

'She's been swimming, she's all wet. Here, why are you so wet?'

'I fell into a stream.'

He was also washed clean. She saw his face in the transfiguring firelight and felt a sharp, extreme, prolonged pain as though the lines of his forehead, nose and jaw were being traced upon her flesh with the point of a knife.

'Are you ill?'

She shook her head.

'Want something to eat?'

She shook her head.

'Best get you some dry clothes, then, or you'll catch your death.'

She crawled against his side and lay there.

'She's showing you affection!' exclaimed Bendigo derisively.

'She's like a little rag doll, she's all limp,' said Jewel curiously. He picked up her arm and dropped it; she allowed her arm to fall uselessly on the ground. He said to her softly: 'What's the matter, love, what's the matter with you?'

'You've given me an endearment,' she said. 'Why did you give me an endearment, what have I done wrong?'

She tried to climb into his jacket and vanish. Mrs Green slapped Jen's bottom.

'You run along, our Jen. I'll just go and see to the Professor girl –'

'No,' said Jewel. 'I'll look after her. She's in a funny mood.'

She tagged along behind him, vacantly biting her fingernails. He took her to the cart where their possessions were packed, scared away a clutch of children who were playing hide and seek among the boxes and bundles and found her a blanket. He undressed her, wrapped her up in the rug, sat her on the tailboard of the cart and seated himself beside her, as if waiting for her to explain. There was still enough light for her to see the close, smooth texture of the skin beneath his

necklace and she ducked forward and kissed the base of his throat
again and again, small, sipping kisses as if she were trying to drink
him down.

'What do you want?'

'I went for a walk and I met the boy.'

'What, the half-wit? Did he go through you, then?'

She nodded and continued to kiss the hollow of his throat. He
laughed, perhaps with genuine amusement.

'Well, what happened, did he get you worked up and then couldn't
finish you off, is that it? Is that why you start making up to me with such
unexpected affection, is that it?'

He continued to laugh in a way that made her wonder if he were
not perhaps within a hair's breadth of killing her; she shook her head.

'What is it, then, did he hurt you?'

She shook her head again. He sighed and remarked casually: 'I'll say
this for you, you aren't half good at getting yourself raped.'

She hit his face and he immediately struck her such a violent blow
on the side of the head that she fell to the ground and lay there, half-
stunned.

'You ever hit me again and I'll beat you to a bloody pulp,' he said
pleasantly, took out his knife and began to pare his fingernails.

When she got her breath back, she said: 'I hate you. Next time you
hit me, I'll take your knife and stab you.'

'I don't think so,' he said; since he was right, she crept back to his
feet, ashamed.

'He says I'm pregnant.' The dark shapes of the carts and the gleams
of firelight reeled about her and the sky with its first few stars now
swung over and now under her. She caught hold of his hand and covered
it with helpless kisses, bruising her lips against the rings.

'Something's got into you, anyway,' he said. 'You've gone out of
your mind.'

'I'm sick.'

'Sick?'

'He's right, I know it.'

'And is it mine?'

'Of course it is.'

'There's no "of course" about it. You go sneaking off and who can tell who tumbles you, you randy bitch.'

'I don't want it. I don't want to stay here.'

'Stop slobbering over my hands.'

'And I'm sick . . .'

'If you stop slobbering over my hands, I'll be kind to you for a while.'

He picked her up; she climbed inside his jacket as much as she could and would have climbed inside his breast to vanish there if such a thing had been possible. Her nostrils were full of wood smoke, the rank richness of horses and the disturbing odour of imperfectly cured animal hide, all of which combined in Jewel's peculiar perfume, but when she looked upwards towards his face, she saw no palpable structure, only a series of hallucinations. Face of a painted devil. Then a cruel, hieratic carving of brown wood and shadow. Then a moving darkness folded, perhaps, in sorrow. But each image was projected successively not on the real face of a living man but against or in opposition to the spare outline of features now traced as with fearful needles on the inside of her brain.

'Who do you see when you see me?' she asked him, burying her own face in his bosom.

'Do you want the truth?'

She nodded.

'The firing squad.'

'That's not the whole truth. Try again.'

'Insatiability,' he said with some bitterness.

'That's oblique but altogether too simple. Once more,' she insisted. 'One more time.'

He was silent for several minutes.

'The map of a country in which I only exist by virtue of the extravagance of my metaphors.'

'Now you're being too sophisticated. And, besides, what metaphors do we have in common?'

He appeared to smile and asked if she were feeling better.

'I am terrified,' she said. 'I've never been so terrified in my whole life.'

'It's not that you're very old,' he pointed out. 'Stand up.'

'I can't.'

'Lie down, then.'

He found some blankets and made her a bed inside the cart, with her head upon a bale of skins. He continued to hold her, however, though abstractedly, and she kissed his throat again and again, reaching under his shirt. He grunted and, not ungently, took away her hand. He was now sunk in thought. She examined his necklaces closely and soon all her attention was concentrated on them. The St Christopher medallion; a string of clear glass beads like eyes of blue; the teeth of a number of wild animals hanging from a strip of leather; three loops of moony pearls which gleamed in the dark; a garland of leaves of gold beaten extremely thin, a beautiful and ancient looking piece.

'I want a necklace,' she said. 'I want your string of beads.'

'Then want must be your master. I'm not giving away my charms and talismans, what would become of me without them?'

It was the necklace of leaves she wanted, such golden leaves as might have grown in Eden itself. As she hung round his neck, herself another necklace, some creakings heralded a visitor to the cart. Donally's shadow fell across them. He held a candle lantern in his hand and carried a flask. The candle was faintly scented with vanilla, a smell at once exotic and domestic.

'A drink,' he said, setting down the fragrant lantern and offering the flask.

'After you,' said Jewel, exercising his usual caution. His tutor drank and Jewel took the flask. Donally clambered in beside them, causing the cart to sway and rock; he cleared a space for himself and settled down uninvited. They were all three so close together they could hear one another breathing. The camp was now in the silence of sleep. Jewel drank and put the mouth of the flask between Marianne's lips.

'Do you good.'

She swallowed a mouthful of the crude liquor and wound around him more closely than before. He covered up her thighs with a fold of blanket.

'Fatherhood,' said the Doctor warmly, introducing the subject without further ado. 'How will you accept the role of father?'

'Complacently.'

'And how shall she cope with that of mother?'

'Only most reluctantly, I should think. Look at her, she's a changed woman; but who knows how long it will last.'

She was half-deafened by the banging of Jewel's heart and far too unhappy to attend to the two men who started to converse above her head in voices which hardly seemed connected with the mouths from which they issued. She kissed her husband's wrist or throat now and then and he absently patted her head as if she were now one of the family and drowsed on his knee like Jen when she was too sleepy to go to bed.

'She says it's my kid. Do you believe her? I guess I'll have to accept the role of father, anyway.'

'I'd believe her, yes. Your brothers wouldn't dare, in fear of whip and noose since you married her, and my son never approached her before today.'

'And him only thirteen years old!' said Jewel in admiration.

'I shall have to keep him chained up all the time, now,' brooded Donally. 'Or else he'll scatter his semen through the tribe like infected dew. I beat him severely when he told me and chained him to a tree. At the moment, he's too affronted to howl.'

'She's really done for, then,' said Jewel, grinning. 'I've really done for her, now.'

'Don't rest on your laurels.'

'What, should I still beware the occult charge of her touch? Are you asleep, Marianne?'

'She isn't. Give her another drink.'

'Doesn't she look young. When I was about her age, I was perfectly innocent, do you remember?'

'Perfectly. Were you scared when you went out raiding, that first time?'

'Not at all. When I painted my face and so on, I became the frightening thing myself and ceased altogether to be anything but the thing I was, an implement for killing people.'

'And she watched you.'

'She converted me into something else by seeing me. Whenever I think of her, when I'm away from her, I always imagine her to be wearing long, black gloves up to her elbows, riding behind me on the saddle, biding her time till the fatal moment.'

'What does the future hold for your child?'

'What does the future hold for yours? Why don't you kill him now, instead of dragging it out?'

Marianne bit his hand. He put his mouth against her ear and said: 'Don't push your luck.'

'What does the future hold for your child if you won't accept your responsibilities?'

'What's that?' demanded Jewel, astonished.

'Would you have punished Precious of your own free will?'

'No.'

'Would you have married her of your own free will?'

'No.'

'Would you create a power structure of your own free will?'

'No.'

'Then how can you hope to be Moses when you won't acknowledge a chosen people?'

'I don't want to be no Moses. And the future is a dream.'

'Hope,' proposed Donally.

'Hope,' repeated Jewel. He contemplated the rings on his fingers for a long time. Then he said:

'Perhaps I should ask her to take me to the Professors, who at least make the pretence of nourishing such a thing. I would resign the tribe to you to do as you pleased with, Doctor, and ride away to the Professors with Marianne as if she were a white flag. Perhaps now is the time to capitulate.'

'Wake her up and ask her what they'd do to you.'

Jewel shook Marianne but she was awake.

'They'd shoot you on sight,' she said.

'What if I sent you first as an emissary, to tell them I was coming and gave myself up freely?'

'They would put you in a cage so everyone could examine you. You'd be an icon of otherness, like a talking beast or a piece of meteorite.'

'If the lion could speak, we would not understand it,' said Donally.

'What if I cunningly revealed my extreme intelligence and excellent though unorthodox education?'

'The Barbarians are Yahoos but the Professors are Laputans,' she said. 'And you haven't been educated according to their requirements.'

'Don't equivocate, answer his question,' said Donally.

'They'd walk around you carefully in case you bit them and clip off your hair and take photographs of the picture on your back, a relic of the survival of Judaeo-Christian iconography, they'd find that very interesting. They'd take away your coat of fur and dress you in a dark suit and set you intelligence tests where you had to match squares with circles and circles with squares. And give you aptitude tests. And manual dexterity tests. And Rorschach blot tests. And introversion/extroversion tests. And blood tests. And many other tests. And everything you did or said would be observed and judged, sleeping and waking, everything, to see how you revealed your differences, every word and gesture studied and annotated until you were nothing but a mass of footnotes with a tiny trickle of text at the top of a page. You would be pressed inside a book. And you'd be lodged probably with psychologists and all the time you'd be a perfect stranger.'

And though all she said was true and would prove quite inimical to the hostile and aggressive sources of his mysterious beauty, still she felt nostalgic for peace and quiet, now she was so ill.

'And you, would you come and visit me in my room or cage, to give me a little charity?'

'No,' she said. 'Not if you were not this thing you are outside.'

'Pass her the flask,' said Donally, well pleased with her.

'But I never really proposed to immolate myself among her people, not in reality,' said Jewel, watching her drink. 'Though what would I become if I made all those concessions for the sake of the child?'

'What will become of you, anyway? You'll get shot on some raid or else in some attack and your remarkable carcass slung into a pit taking my masterpieces with it, more's the pity.'

'Everywhere I go, I'm doomed to be nothing but an exhibit,' said Jewel.

'I am an intellectual myself, what else do you expect from intellectuals; we are accustomed to examine things and scarcely bother ourselves about the hurt feelings of the things we examine, why should we? She's passing out.'

'No, she's still kissing me. Have a bit of dignity, girl, pull yourself together. Embrace your destiny with style, that's the important thing. Pretend you're Eve at the end of the world.'

'Lilith,' said Donally, pedantically. 'Call her Lilith.'

'That's a bad heredity. Besides, I always thought of Lilith as kind of mature.'

'She's a little Lilith.'

She said to Jewel: 'You are so beautiful, I think you must be true.'

'That's a fallacy,' snapped Donally.

'But I think that, in the long run, I shall be forced to trust appearances. When I was a little girl, we played at heroes and villains but now I don't know which is which any more, nor who is who, and what can I trust if not appearances? Because nobody can teach me which is which nor who is who because my father is dead.'

'You'll have to learn for yourself, then,' said Jewel. 'Don't we all.'

'Give me your son and I'll turn him into the Tiger Boy.'

'He wouldn't survive it.'

'I've perfected my technique since then, through the years; I wouldn't harm him. Tattooing is the first of the post-apocalyptic arts, its materials are flesh and blood.'

He gave his lecture theatre cough but Jewel interrupted him.

'It's going to be a little girl, anyway. It's going to be a small, black, spiteful little girl and I'll cut my heart out for her to play with, if she wants it. Why did you try to poison her and me, that time? Was it another example of your diabolical artistry? Like when you killed my father?'

'He was an old man who wanted to live for ever but he had a cancer. You don't want to understand anything.'

'Do something for me,' said Jewel slowly.

'Yes. All right,' said Donally suspiciously.

'Set your son free and throw away his chains.'

'Why?'

'To show me you didn't mean to kill my father and you mixed up the drugs.'

'How illogical,' said Donally. He stood up, mounted on a box and urinated over the side of the cart. Then he resumed his position beside Jewel and slid his arm about him.

'I regard you as my proper son.'

'Did you become my father when you killed my father? What, did you eat him?'

'I assumed responsibility for you.'

'What, trying to kill me, too, on and off for ten years?'

'I taught you all I knew.'

'Caution, you certainly taught me caution. And genetics, metaphysics, some conjuring tricks and a few quotations from old books in dead languages.'

'It's not too late to learn from me. I'll give you a future, if you'd only listen. I could make you so terrifying the bends of the road would straighten out with fright as you rode down. I'll make you a politician and you could become the King of all the Yahoos and all the Professors, too; they need a myth as passionately as anyone else, they need a hero. Tamburlaine the Scourge of Asia conquered half the world by the time he reached your age but you can quickly make up for lost time.'

'Set him free.'

'Who?'

'Your son. My brother, if you are my father.'

'I'm frightened of him,' said Donally after a long silence.

A shivering howl rose through the dark air and Marianne raised her head from Jewel's breast to listen.

'Set him free and I'll do whatever you want. I'll even learn to play the conquering hero, if you set him free.'

'But what would happen then?'

'If you refuse, you'd better take him to the Professors so they can cage him and give him blood tests.'

Donally shook the flask and heard no liquid rattle within. He dropped it on the floor of the cart.

'Take him and leave him?'

'No. Take him away but never come back yourself. Go home. I'm tired of you.'

'Don't be hasty. Consider.'

'How can I possibly trust you if you're frightened of something? Take your spells and prayers elsewhere and take away that bloody snake which signifies nothing. I don't want you any more.'

'But you still need me.'

'Set your son free and you can stay.'

'What will you do if I go away? Will you continue to rob and plunder or do you propose to settle and plant gardens?'

'She's clever. She'll think of something.'

'I'll leave you,' she said furiously. 'As soon as the baby is born.'

'You'll never,' said Jewel contemptuously. 'You're creaming for me now, this very minute.'

He thrust his hand between her legs but she said: 'That doesn't mean I wouldn't leave you.'

'Neither does it,' he agreed. 'But it suggests you might find going more difficult than coming.'

'The candle is dying,' observed Donally. 'I'll go to bed.'

'I do believe we've come to the parting of the ways, at last.'

'Do you?' said Donally. He stood up and stretched. He appeared to reach to the top of the sky and the young man and woman cowered at his feet but this impression lasted only for a moment. He swung over the side of the cart and was gone, leaving only a burned-out candle lantern and an empty flask. Now only the stars and the cold, pale, crescent moon gave out a phantom light.

'Everybody is asleep,' said Jewel. 'But my poor brother has his back on fire. Was it his son or Precious howling, do you think?'

Her fingers were all twisted in his golden leaves; suddenly he wrenched them away from her and said, in as cool and rational a voice as she had ever heard: 'I am desperate; I am at the end of my tether.'

'Don't leave me by myself!'

But he had already shoved her against the sacks and was gone so she was quite alone with no protection at all, under the sky. Under the sky, the villagers slept sweetly behind barbed wire and armed watch towers which kept those on the outside from getting inside and those on the inside from getting out, except for this one female renegade who now stayed wide awake while the travellers slept rough upon the open heath and the Out People in subterranean dens slept, wild beasts slept in acrid dens and birds slept upon the sleeping trees so the ball of the world spinning in space was wholly possessed by a trustful sleep which rendered everything defenceless, a communal defencelessness which obliterated the differences between them all under the sky, which pressed down inexorably on the fragile, mutable structures beneath it like a heavy cover crushing all to extinction. The idea of the round world became flat as the palm of Marianne's hand and shook itself, shrank and changed until it became no more than the splintered wood beneath her, some textures of coarse wool and fur and the little world of herself which contained all that it was possible for her to know. As she gathered herself together, the sky returned to its proper place and Jewel came back. She was surprised; she thought he had gone for good.

'I've brought you a present, a necklace, what you wanted.'

He carried several coils of cold metal; it was the boy's chain. He fell down and feverishly tried to bind her up with it but she easily disengaged her arms.

'Jewel Lee Bradley, you scabby robber, you're drunk again.'

He asked her her own question of earlier in the evening, though with far greater intensity than she.

'What do you see when you see me?'

'I see your face when I close my eyes though I would much rather not.'

'I thought as much,' he said and let the chain slide to the ground. Then they went to sleep, for they were both exhausted. The next morning, he sent her to Mrs Green, who left off stirring the porridge, took her into the relative privacy of the ruined barn, undressed her and examined her.

'You're about three months gone, I reckon,' she said.

Green juicy weeds flourished shoulder high around them and cast delicate green shadows on Marianne's breasts.

'Have you been missing your periods and all? Why didn't you tell me?'

'I didn't notice.'

Mrs Green hugged her, kissed her and allowed her to dress herself. The chips of mirror on Marianne's shirt shone with the refreshed light of morning like many small eyes opened after sleep.

'You must take care of yourself, now; you can't go trudging along in the dust and muck, it's not right.'

'I shall go wherever he goes,' said Marianne composedly.

'Is it as bad as that, dear?' said Mrs Green with melancholy satisfaction and kissed her again. Marianne realized the woman had quite misinterpreted her and thought she meant she wanted to be Jewel's shadow for ever; she was about to correct her when she saw a flash of scarlet through the doorway.

It was the boy, unchained, dressed up in Jewel Lee Bradley's wedding coat of rotten scarlet silk which reached down stiffly to his bare feet. He was eating the meat off a chop bone. He wandered past the door, kicking the hem of the coat in front of him at each step, followed by a lean, balding brown dog who curiously sniffed the hem of his robe. He looked extremely happy, he beamed like the sun, which that morning shone with the tremulous light of the end of the year.

7

While Mrs Green was examining Marianne, Jewel went down to the stream and threw the boy's chain into the water. When he returned to the camp, the Doctor sought him out and attempted to shoot him with a pearl-handled revolver but he missed. Jewel knocked him down. When Mrs Green and Marianne came out of the barn, they found Donally lying on his back in the grass beside the apple tree where Precious had been whipped. Jewel stood beside him, running his thumb down the edge of his knife and the entire tribe had gathered in a wide, wonder-struck and apprehensive circle round the fallen figure of the shaman.

'I've not killed him yet,' said Jewel to Marianne. 'I wanted to ask your opinion.'

'The porridge is burning,' said Mrs Green and retreated to her cooking fire.

'Your foster-mother has deserted you,' said Dr Donally. His dark glasses lay in smashed fragments beside him and he blinked a little in the cool light of morning.

'A public evisceration?' said Jewel to Marianne but she knocked the knife out of his hand.

'Look at them all, watching. Be careful, they respect him.'

'You listen to her,' said Donally approvingly. 'She's no fool.'

'Keep quiet, you.'

It was like a parody of the performance of justice, only the audience had not the least idea what was happening or who was to be feared.

'Let him go,' said Marianne. 'Put him on his donkey and send him away. Best not to murder him.'

'Is it wise to let him loose?'

'The wild beasts might eat him and do our job for us, in the natural state.'

'You'll be all alone without me,' said the Doctor to Jewel. 'All alone for ever and ever.'

Jewel kicked him. The boy appeared, red as a rose, with his arms full of old man's beard and the feathery seeding heads of purple loosestrife; he took in the situation at a glance and, convulsed with mirth, scattered the soft, grey fruits over his father.

'I see you ironically covered his nakedness with your wedding coat, Jewel,' said Donally appreciatively.

'I won't have you using that name which was given me out of affection.' He put away the knife with an air of decision. 'But you can go, so then you won't need to name me by anything.'

The boy danced backwards as Donally reared up, shedding a drifting cloud of purple blossom.

'See how he treats his oldest friend!' he declaimed to the wild gathering.

'They'll think what I tell them to think. That's my privilege.'

'Once I'm gone, no doubt you'll start taking my advice; but you'll be like an Eskimo trying to drive a train, you'll be impotent.'

'There's mud all over you but I won't let you clean yourself; go as you are.'

'Am I allowed to take my books?'

'I'll burn them.'

'My drugs?'

'I'll poison the nearest stream with them and all the fish will die.'

'My son?'

'If he wants to go, he can go. Otherwise, he can stay.'

'That's magnanimous,' said Donally unpleasantly.

Johnny brought the donkey, ready saddled, and the Doctor mounted it with all his former *élan*. He bent down and pronounced his farewell in such loud and oracular tones everyone in the camp would hear it.

'She shall have a vile childbed culminating in a monstrous birth and ultimately she will betray you in circumstances of unbelievable horror.'

Lightning should have flashed but did not.

'Get going,' said Jewel. He was battered and unkempt. He had neglected to duly braid the locks that hung in jags and dags down his shoulders and he was barefoot and ragged, though shining as always with glass, gold and precious stones, the Prince of Darkness but no gentleman and surrounded by silence. Donally's donkey lowered its head and cropped the grass; Donally abandoned his prophetic manner and instead childishly implored, in an intimate whisper:

'Give me one last look at my masterpiece.'

'I think not,' said Jewel.

Marianne was afraid one or other of the company would break forward in defence of the magician, that a man would raise a rifle and shoot Jewel or a woman throw a stone at him, but nobody moved. Donally took his flute from an inner pocket and began to play sweet and penetrating music as if this were his last card and irresistible. Jewel snatched the flute from his lips and broke it across his knee. Donally petulantly threw up his hands and sighed.

'Take me away,' he said. 'Throw me out. Throw out art, throw out culture, throw out wit and humour.'

Johnny's eyes were fixed on Jewel, perhaps trying to learn some secret formula of expulsion. Marianne thought: 'I will never trust Johnny.' A smell of scorched porridge hung in the air; Mrs Green, watching nervously from beside her fire, neglected to stir.

'Watch out nobody shoots me in the back,' said Jewel to Johnny. After a moment, Johnny took his rifle and covered the crowd. Jewel slapped the donkey's rump and took hold of its bridle; Marianne went with them but Donally's son had lost interest in whatever was happening and now wandered off without a backward glance. The donkey stepped daintily between the sprawling briars on the ground, batting its spoon-shaped ears.

'I shall burn the snake, alive or dead, and your mask and feather cloak,' said Jewel. 'It will be as if you never existed.'

'Don't be too sure of that,' said the Doctor. 'I've made my mark. And shall you really settle and plant gardens? You'll be an idiot slave of nature, you'll farm poisons, you'll never be free.'

'I am perfectly indifferent as regards the future. She can do a bit of thinking from time to time, perhaps.'

They arrived at the green road and stood looking at one another, in a sudden last uncertainty as to where their three allegiances lay, for the young man and his tutor had the strange attachment of years between them, the girl and her husband the bemused attraction of a sense of fatality and the girl and the magician the bond of a common language. And the girl and the young man, also, each suffered from the loss of a father.

'Come with me, both of you,' said Donally. 'I shall take both of you under my protection. I shall go to the Professors and tell them you are my son and daughter-in-law, snatched from the arboreal innocence of the forest. Then they will treat you with that awed respect, tinged with circumspection, which the savants of eighteenth-century France reserved for the Hurons and the Iroquois.'

Jewel hid his face behind his hands, confronted by this new, extra-ordinary possibility which rendered him speechless. At last he said:

'I can't help myself. I'm incorruptible.'

'Marianne, come with me by yourself. Consider your researches into the *mœurs* of savage tribes completed.'

'So that is what I've been doing!' she thought.

Jewel watched her between his fingers. She was caught between the beams of their eyes and vacillated.

'Not yet,' she temporized. 'They're not completed yet.'

Donally's face was suffused with such evil and baleful fury he grew as mottled as his own mask.

'Well, then,' he said, 'you've made your bed and you must lie on it.'

With that, he moved off. He was so enormous he dwarfed the beast beneath him and distance rendered him down to a manageable size only very, very slowly. Marianne sat down on the bank while Jewel stood impassively in the middle of the road until Donally vanished round the bend. Just then, his son flung himself precipitously past Marianne and down the bank in a slither of pebbles; he was panting, he had been running fast.

'Which way?'

Jewel pointed. The boy hurtled off like a scarlet bullet or a red ball propelled energetically along a green cloth in the direction which his father had taken until he, too, vanished. After a pause, Jewel began to laugh, shaking his head in bewilderment.

'Blood is thicker than water,' offered Marianne by way of a tentative explanation. 'Can we live in the forest by ourselves?'

Until she spoke, she had no idea she would say this; when she perceived she and her Jewel were, in some way, related to one another she was filled with pain for her idea of her own autonomy might, in fact, be not the truth but a passionately held conviction. However, might not such a conviction serve her as well as a proven certainty? When she realized she had begun to think in such circuitous slogans as Donally might paint on his wall, she was abashed and fixed her eyes on the carpet of weeds in the roadway.

'How would we live?'

'In the ruins. Or a cave.'

'And you'd have this baby all by yourself? Cut its string and wash off the grease and all, if I was killed? What would you do if I was hurt, would you know what to do? And nobody to get you things to eat and the Out People shooting off their arrows at you? And my brothers out looking for me with guns and nooses because I betrayed them?'

She could think of no immediate answer and shrugged.

'We'll go back, now.'

'And do what?'

'Eat.'

'Then?'

'Go on.'

'Where?'

'To the sea.'

'And then?'

'You talk too much,' he said. The blue medal was a ring of sky at his throat.

'St Christopher was the patron saint of travellers, when they had such things,' she told him in a falsely encouraging voice.

'There are more ghosts on the highway than anywhere else, such as ghosts of machines running along by themselves. Here, what did you do with your wedding ring?'

'I don't know. It fell off.'

'In that case, how can you expect me to trust you?'

Since he reconstructed the world solely in terms of imagery, she found it hard to understand him. When they got back to the camp, he carried out all his promises to Donally. He burned the books, emptied the drugs, burned the herbs and destroyed every relic which the Doctor had left behind. It was indeed a dead snake, and stuffed. He took it from its cage and cut it open so the sawdust spilled out in front of everybody before he burned it. The books opened and blackened in the flames like trapped crows and the feather robe took wings and flew away on fire. All that remained of Donally was dust and ashes. The sullen puzzlement of the tribesmen lent their silence a new and terrible quality.

'Soon they'll start making the sign against the evil eye when they see you,' said Marianne.

'Then I shall begin to exercise authority,' he replied.

'He's out of his mind,' said Mrs Green as if she hoped the reason was as simple as that. 'He doesn't know what he's doing.'

'They think I've bewitched you,' said Marianne. 'You've put us both at risk.'

He filled a sack with Donally's pots and messes and took it down to the stream, where its contents followed the chain to the bottom. The bonfire was still smouldering when the tribe took to the road about the middle of the day, when his house-cleaning was finished. Wherever Jewel went, that day, he had a brother on either side of him and they looked like a bodyguard. Precious was too ill to ride on horseback and lay stretched out, bandaged, beside Mrs Green in her cart, moaning at the jolts and now and then becoming delirious but Mrs Green was happy to have another child again. Marianne walked beside them but continually refused to climb up out of the dirt. The wind grew cold, fresh and very lively; it blew white gusts of seagulls who gave forth mysterious cries above them.

'What is the sea like, Mrs Green?'

'A whole lot of empty water, shifting up and down twice a day. Otherwise, much the same as anywhere else. But it is too far to reach the fishing village, today, owing to his being so late in starting out, due to his whims. We shall have to camp somewhere along the road.'

They came to an artificial gulley of pocked stone with, on either side, some low, grey, stone buildings with several rooms still solid enough to shelter them. Bushes and trees now grew where the rails had been.

There was a room full of rusted levers with a clock stuck in the wall; its glass face hung loosely away from a dial all woven over by spiders. The door of this room lay flat on the broken paving stones before it but the roof was still sound. Night came; that confusion between need and desire against which she had been warned consumed her. If it was only that she desired him, then it became a simple situation which she could perfectly resolve while continuing to despise him. But if he was necessary to her, that constituted a wholly other situation which raised a constellation of miserable possibilities each one indicating that, willy nilly, she would be changed. As a result of this infuriating confusion, she raked her nails across his back with such insensate vehemence she broke the skin deeply in several places, as if trying to tear the picture off his back. She dipped her fingertips in the deep, blood-filled runnels and twisted round to taste the blood; it tasted much like any other blood, no especial flavour.

'What else did you expect?' he demanded.

He lay as still as the clock which had not ticked for more years than he had been alive, or his father before him, but she knew he was not asleep. She wondered if he was waiting for somebody to creep up and knife him in the night but nothing moved; only the dry twigs rustled where the trains had run. She kept to her own side of the mattress and did not sleep, either; she held her hands against her belly and tried to feel the shape of the child down there which knitted its flesh and blood out of her own in the artificial night of the womb while there was nothing she could do about it. After a long time, Jewel got up and pulled on his clothes. She waited until he reached the door before she said:

'Where are you going?'

He started visibly in the colourless starlight. She saw the whites of his eyes.

'Where are you going?'

'To the sea.'

'How far is it?'

'Over the hill. I've been here before.'

It had now become very cold and she furred herself up to go out with him but they both went barefoot. They threaded their way past tents of skin and dead fires of black sticks and stepped over the stretched bodies of sleeping dogs. Blue was on guard outside the camp but lay asleep under a blanket with his arms around a girl.

'Caught red-handed stealing his peculiar honey,' said Jewel and made to wake him but Marianne put her hand on his arm and stopped him, for the young man and girl, sleeping, seemed to her such a peaceful and beautiful sight that nothing under the moon which saw them would want to harm them. Although this might not be what she really believed; she might wish, in her heart, for the Out People or Soldiers or wild beasts to arrive in packs and overwhelm the sleeping camp, and her sudden access of sentimentality serve only as a screen to conceal this real motive from herself. She wondered if this was the motive Jewel imputed to her; or if it was also his, for he shrugged and they left the illicit pair as they had found them.

He went off before her over the tussocky grass. She could only see him dimly like his own shadow, as he went up the hill-side and then his outline, against the sky. She followed him and found the grass ended and the sand-dunes began. She had never seen or touched sand before and scooped up a handful to sniff it. It smelled dry and unnatural. Her shifting footsteps slurred and whispered. The dunes exuded a pale radiance of their own; their low, round shapes, sprouting here and there a little coarse grass, were so suggestive of the forms of life they might at any moment shake themselves into one giant elemental of unknown voluptuousness. The thin crust of sand crumbled beneath her bare feet; spiny thistles so small she could not see them in the dark pricked her feet. Jewel appeared again on the crest of a dune; he chinked. When she arrived where he stood, she saw the sea.

Quilted flats of shining sand stretched before her, for the tide was out, and, retiring, had left behind it at high-water line, just beneath them, ankle-deep heaps of weed, beds of broad, dirty shells as large as a hand, driftwood and all manner of marine detritus. Jewel ran forward, down the side of the dune, across the beach and out towards the distant corrugations of sea, in which the little new moon moved. He stopped where the small waves broke with a secret sound. Less impetuously, Marianne followed him.

Before them and around them were all the wonders of the seashore, to which Marianne could scarcely put a single name, though everything had once been scrupulously named. The fans, fronds, ribbons, wreaths, garlands and lashes of weed had once been divided into their separate families, wracks, tangles, dulses, etc. Purse sponge, slime sponge, breadcrumb sponge, blood red sponge; tube sea squirt, rough sea squirt, gooseberry sea squirt, star sea squirt (or golden star). Rag worms, lug worms, tube worms. The soft corals and sea anemones, known as dead men's fingers, snake locks, wartlet or gem anemone, the globehorn, the daisy anemone, cup coral, sea firs, sea oaks. The spiny skinned family of echinoderms, which include the brittle stars, feather stars, the sea cucumbers with their mouth fringe of whispy gills and the sea lilies which have ten feathery arms waving in the water. The jellyfish. And innumerable other names.

Losing their names, these things underwent a process of uncreation and reverted to chaos, existing only to themselves in an unstructured world where they were not formally acknowledged, becoming an ever-widening margin of undifferentiated and nameless matter surrounding the outposts of man, who no longer made himself familiar with these things or rendered them authentic in his experience by the gift of naming. Jewel and Marianne walked along the beach of this wide, unfrequented bay not as if they were discovering it, or exploring it, but like visitors who have arrived too late, without an introduction, are unsure of their welcome but, nevertheless, determined to brave it out.

So they made their way towards the jutting spit of land at the tip of the crescent of sand. Marianne trod in his crisply delineated footprints, which were already filling with water. If he and she left the tribe, they would become Out People and surrender to namelessness, if the worst came to the worst; but, at best, they might begin a new subspecies of man who would live in absolute privacy in secret caves, accompanied only by danger of death, imbibing a suitable indifference to the outside with its mother's milk. This fearless and rational breed would eschew such mysteries as the one now forcing her to walk behind the figure on the shore, dark as the negative of a photograph, and preventing her from returning home alone. Therefore she might not be able to teach his children how to be absolutely indifferent, since she herself was so bad at it, and her whole plan crumbled to nothing. She began to speak with considerable bitterness.

'You are the most remarkable thing I ever saw in all my life. Not even in pictures had I seen anything like you, nor read your description in books, you with your jewels, paints, furs, knives and guns, like a phallic and diabolic version of female beauties of former periods. What I'd like best would be to keep you in preserving fluid in a huge jar on the mantelpiece of my peaceful room, where I could look at you and imagine you. And that's the best place for you, you walking masterpiece of art, since the good Doctor educated you so far above your station you might as well be an exhibit for intellectuals to marvel at as anything else. You, you're nothing but the furious invention of my virgin nights.'

He allowed her a single, curious smile but said not one word in reply and they reached the headland while she nagged him as cunningly as she could. But she fell silent when she saw what lay beyond the headland.

Here was a time-eaten city up to its ears in the sea, its towers, domes and roofs so mingled with their own shadows and reflections that all seemed to hang in mid-air, among clouds of night and waning stars. Long ago the sea wrenched apart the massive blocks of an esplanade, though these were tons in weight and clasped together; then the sea swirled through the abandoned thoroughfares nibbling, gobbling, gulping and digesting stone, brick, stucco, metal and concrete. Now incurious fish swam in bedrooms where submerged mirrors reflected faces no more, only the mazy dance of wrack and wreckage; fish swam through ocean-gone ovens and out again, uncooked; fish in their native element went gaping through ballroom, store and hotel in this town which had once been a resort built for purposes of pleasure. Since the wind had dropped during the night, the waves made no more noise than their own breathing.

Prominent among the minarets, spires and helmets of wrought iron which protruded from the waters was an enormous clock whose hands stood still at the hour of ten though it was, of course, no longer possible to tell whether this signified ten in the morning or ten at night. This clock was held in the arms and supported on the forward-jutting stomach of a monstrous figure in some kind of plasterwork which appeared to spring on tiptoe from the lagoon like the *genius loci*, since the plinth which bore it was completely submerged. It was the figure of a luxuriously endowed woman scantily clad in a one-piece bathing costume which, at the top, scarcely contained the rising swell of mountainous breasts in the shadowy cleft of which sea birds nested so the whole figure was splashed with white droppings. In daylight, this woman's garment still retained streaks of the cheerful blue with which it had been painted, just as the flesh was still stained here and there a vivid pink, but night bleached these colours out. The head, equipped with exuberant, shoulder-length curls, was thrown back in erotic ecstasy and, though partially worn away by the salty winds, the face clearly displayed a gigantic pair of lips twisted in a wide, joyous smile revealing a fine set of plaster teeth. The eyes used to shine since blue electric light bulbs had been set in the sockets and bulbs of different colours had also surrounded the clock but these were now memories which nobody remembered. Near this figure, the uppermost part of a wheel of gigantic size rose above the smug and serene sea.

Beyond the drowned town, the land grew high and there towered a cliff so tall it would be many centuries before the sea subdued it though, in course of time, this was bound to happen, as the breakers hurled themselves against its face. The grey sea horses which now looked so quiescent would grow violent in the equinoctial storms; they would assault the cliffs not merely with their own impetus but also with missiles concealed inside them, boulders, pebbles and abrasive sand. They would drive the air before them and force it against the cliff; even the air was its enemy, for, released by the sea, it exploded, ripping parts of the cliff away. The waves would in this way undermine the cliffs until the upper part finally collapsed.

But this date was well in the future and, upon the cliff, a white tower glistened like a luminous finger pointing to heaven. It was a lighthouse. Its light was put out, like the woman's eyes, but here it stayed and if there were no longer any storm-tossed mariners to give thanks for its helpful beams, yet, functionless as it was, it was intransigent. To Marianne, it looked the twin of the white tower in which she had been born and she was very much moved for, though neither tower any longer cast a useful light, both still served to warn and inform of surrounding dangers. Thus this tower glimpsed in darkness symbolized and clarified her resolution; abhor shipwreck, said the lighthouse, go in fear of unreason. Use your wits, said the lighthouse. She fell in love with the integrity of the lighthouse. It did not occur to her that her companion might regard her as more representative of the culture of the carrier of the defunct clock nor could she have understood how this was possible, for the psychology of the outcast was a closed book to her and, besides, he had never learned to write.

It grew very dark as the stars went out one by one. Behind them, the tide was beginning to creep back over the exposed strand; out of curiosity, she wanted to ask Jewel if the lewd clock-bearer were fully hidden at high tide but found she could not break the pentacle of his continuous, black silence. He turned back the way they had come and led her into the dunes till the headland hid the town in the sea or the sea in the town and they were also out of sight of the approaching hem of water. He knelt and began to scrabble a depression in the sand.

'What on earth are you doing, now?'

'Digging a hole, crawling into it and sleeping.'

He lay down half-buried in the sand like a black fox which has gone to earth and she sat beside him. She watched his closed eyelids flicker at the passage of the dreams beneath them until she experienced such a vibrating intensity of tenderness and concern for him she jumped up and ran away, discontented until two or three tumuli separated them. The conurbation had formerly spread out fingers of small houses behind the dunes; she found herself high enough to see the rotten concrete sunk in foliage, a horrid but natural growth as if ruin had been the original blueprint and men and women had lived here only in a necessary but intermediate stage of the execution of the grand design. It was impossible to tell where houses began and trees ended. When she saw a stir of movement in a ruined house, she thought her eyes were deceiving her and when she saw a lion leap through the window hole of a chalet bungalow, she thought she was asleep and dreaming.

She had never seen a lion before. It looked exactly like the pictures of itself; though darkness washed its colours off, she saw its mane and tasselled tail which flicked about as it moved out of the edge of shadow on to the dune. It paused to snuff the air, bayed softly and resumed its sinuous progression across the sand. Immediately she returned to the place where she had left Jewel though it was now some distance away and the idea that she played hide and seek with a lion in order, perhaps, to die beside her husband seemed to her utterly preposterous even as she felt her heart contract within her to think of the terrible, innocent paw snatching away her husband's skin and he bereft of life.

The lion reached Jewel before her. She cleared a ridge of sand and saw the lion's blunt, noble profile bent over the man, sweeping his hidden shape with the mane that hung from its great, domed head. The world ceased to whirl and the sea to move; the shore was now the lion's home and she and the man were intruders who could only survive by imitating the stillness of the sand itself, to freeze in silence, attempting to deceive the devouring beast by the pretence of not-being. The ancestors of this lion came over the sea in cages to delight and instruct the children of domestic times; she watched it and was instructed. Its eyes glowed more steadily than candle flames and Jewel would feel its warm presence close and amorous; it was a most seductive death. It investigated the man thoroughly with nose and tongue. Its tail twitched from side to side.

Then it raised its head and yawned immensely, prey to an infinite boredom. Jewel lay as he had lain before the fire; if it bit him it would find no flesh inside his clothes so the lion sniffed him over one more time and wandered off, indifferent. Back it went to the forest, such miraculous, slinking grace, joints and muscles loosely and easily moving beneath the skin; it took its own time, which was very slow.

Marianne waited until it disappeared among the dunes and then she waited some more but still Jewel did not move. She waited again, and again, until she saw the sand held a paler glow and, looking behind her, she saw some hints of dawn in the sky, some breaks of blonde cloud. At that, she went to him. He was dark as a calcined statue but his eyes were open; she recalled pictures of the Ancient Egyptians who used to paint figures of the dead with their eyes open so they could see the way to the next world.

'Gypsy is a corruption of the word, "Egyptian",' she told him in a cool voice, to keep at a distance from him.

'My mother's family, the Lees, they were gypsies, whatever that was, before the war. They traded scrap metal, or so my father said, and were wonderfully surprised at the amount of scrap metal the war provided until they realized there was no one left to trade it with and became chagrined. Are you real or am I dreaming you or did a lion come and lick my face?'

'A lion came. I saw it.'

'They must be breeding in the forest. At first they were very rare but soon will be an everyday hazard. I often wondered what it would be like to be the quarry as well as the hunter and lie in the undergrowth in ecstatic dread, harkening to my own intrepid footsteps. It licked my face and went away.'

'Yes, it was remarkable.'

There was no help for it; she knelt beside him and put her arms around him. But when she tried to slide her tongue into his mouth, he pushed her away. In the forest, the lion roared like sweet thunder.

'I don't believe there'll be a dawn this morning,' he said.

'It's started already. Everything is as it should be.'

But one by one he took the rings off his fingers and buried them deep in the sand. Then the rings from his ears.

'Why are you doing that?'

'Go back. Go back and go to sleep.'

'What about you?'

'Leave me alone.'

'Do you want the lion to eat me?'

'He's gone away, he won't do you no harm.'

'I'll go if you want,' she said perfidiously.

'Don't look behind you.'

She lay behind a dune and spied on him. He walked back down to the water's edge. She followed him. The light was bleak and mean, promising a day of rain and clouds. He took the chains and amulets from his neck and laid them on the surface of the smallest waves of the incoming tide, which first washed them farther up the beach, then briefly floated them and then a big wave, a seventh wave, took them in its hollow and they vanished into the heart of the sea. Alone on the sickle of sand, Jewel looked as tiny and as inconsequent as a cast shell. He walked into the sea.

He walked slowly but the incoming waters took him to their changing breasts and the backward tug of the waves made him stumble but he persevered. His hair floated out on the water and soon only his head was visible, as if it had been decapitated and set on an endless platter of ridged silver. She precipitated herself across the beach, threw off her jacket, leapt into the freezing water and caught hold of him. He fought her with all his considerable strength.

Both lost their footing and wrestled in a contention of air and water. He swore, gasped and tried to drag her down and drown her but she was too agile for him and the water overcame him, anyway; he choked and went limp. The incoming tide thrust them up the shore and she pulled him across the sand by his hair till they were out of its reach. He had fainted. His flesh was wet and cold as that of a marine creature. She lay on top of him, covered him and warmed him until he returned to consciousness, moaned and hit her with extraordinary violence, so she was flung quite away from him. He crawled some small distance and vomited up a good deal of water. Soaked and aching, Marianne remembered she was pregnant and screamed with rage.

'That's the second time you've hit me. How could you hit me, at such a time. If you ever hit me again, something terrible will happen to you.'

'I told you not to look back.'

It was bitterly cold. She found her dry jacket and wrapped herself up. He was shaking and weeping but she allowed him to lurch upright, unaided, because she disliked him so passionately. He appeared to resent the ghastly indignity of her rescue more than anything. The night was over; he deserted her. She let him go on ahead of her, back to the camp, and followed his footprints afterwards, shivering and muttering vindictively to herself. In the camp, they were lighting the first fires.

She went into the room with the levers, took off her wet clothes and lay down. She was exhausted and numb with cold. To her surprise, Mrs Green brought her a bowl of porridge and stood over her with arms akimbo as she ate it.

'What happened?' asked Mrs Green. 'He looks like hell.'

Marianne ate another spoonful placidly before she replied.

'He tried to drown himself. When I got him out of the sea, he hit me. Look at the bruise.'

She displayed her shoulder.

'Oh, my God,' said Mrs Green. 'And you in the family way, as well.'

'It will be his fault if I miscarry,' said Marianne smugly and repeated these words in a louder voice as she saw him approach the door. Water streamed from his hair and his soaked clothes stuck to him, the gaunt survivor of a shipwreck, his eyes momentarily blind as pearls. Mrs Green stood squarely before the girl in order to protect her but Jewel carried only a torn scrap of paper in his hand.

'She'll have to read it aloud for me.'

He placed the note in her hand and sank down beside her. She moved away so that no part of her would touch him and examined the message, which comprised a few scribbled words on the back of one of Dr Donally's engraved visiting cards. The card was creased and dusty.

'He says: "SAVE ME".' She had expected some gnomic aphorism. She was disappointed. Jewel pulled a blanket over his head and coughed.

'Dry yourself,' said Mrs Green. 'Your health is so precarious.'

'He wants a rescue, see,' said Jewel heavily. He was so waterlogged all his movements were in slow motion as if he had remained at the bottom of the sea and brought this environment on land with him.

'How did you get this note, anyway?'

'His son brought it. He just came and started eating porridge from the pot with his fingers and he said some Soldiers surprised his father and loaded him with irons; so much for the persuasive powers of his silver tongue. But the boy hisself, he got away, perhaps flew.'

'It's lies,' said Marianne. 'And you know it.'

He slowly began to rub himself dry with the blankets. Mrs Green stooped and felt his forehead.

'You're in a fever.'

'I'm on fire,' he said. 'There must be something wrong with the sea.'

Though the water drops ran down his arms, he seemed to crackle with fever; Marianne felt this fever heat beside her and did not know what to do.

'Does he expect me to rescue him after I expelled him?'

'So it would seem,' said Marianne.

'And am I really burning?' he asked as if he could not trust the evidence of his own senses.

'You are.'

'I must go and talk to my brothers.'

'Stay here and keep still,' said Mrs Green.

Marianne felt a movement under her heart like a fish plopping in a pool. She dug her nails into her palms to create a counter-irritant to her tenderness but, all the same, she said:

'Don't go.'

'It's easier said than done; I am nothing but the immediate promptings of my conscience –'

The brothers came to find him, anyway. Johnny, Bendigo, Jacob and Blue, for Precious was still too much hurt to move. They darkened the room with their presence; they stood around the mattress like four handsome and anonymous young trees.

'Get up,' said Johnny. 'She's bewitched you, it's her that made you turn him out. You can't keep your hands off her, can you, she's eating you. You aren't the man you were.'

Johnny had four knives of different sizes, a rifle on his shoulder and a revolver in his belt. There was blood of slaughtered animals on his furs.

'He's ill,' said Mrs Green.

'He is far too ill to go chasing that charlatan,' said Marianne.

'He hasn't the time to be ill,' said Johnny. 'He's got his job to do. You just shut up, you bitch.'

'I shall not shut up!' she shouted. At that, to her astonishment, Johnny took a few scared backward steps and made the sign against the evil eye. She felt the beginnings of a sense of power.

'But I shall get up and I must get up,' said Jewel. 'I shall go and look for my tutor although it is most likely a trap to delude me and I shall be killed and you with me, Johnny, Jacob, you also, Bendigo, and Blue who can't even be trusted to keep watch; I hope I shall be able to take you all with me. And we shall all together make a beautiful dive into nothing, we –'

'You'll stay with me and father your child.'

'What?' exclaimed Johnny.

'She is,' said Mrs Green with fat contentment.

'Now leave me alone to paint my face and tire my head and find a window to look out of –'

The Lees were Old Believers. Mrs Green, as if mesmerized, took up his weird thread.

'– and the little dogs came and ate up everything but the palms of her hands.'

'If you go out after Donally, I shall leave you.'

'See if I care.'

The Doctor's son appeared, eating bread. The adventures of the past day and night had reduced his coat to shreds.

'What are you going to do?' he asked Jewel as if continuing a conversation begun elsewhere.

'Paint my face. Fetch my jars of paint, watch me turn into the nightmare.'

Johnny signalled to the others and they were gone as suddenly as they had come. The boy went, also, to root about in their possessions until he found the paints.

'When the Soldiers see you coming, they will think you are the devil incarnate, riding a black horse.'

'They are the devils, with their glass faces. One cannot escape the consequences of one's appearance.'

'It is the true appearance of neither of you.'

'But it's true as long as one or the other of us wants to believe it.'

'You're not a human being at all, you're a metaphysical proposition.'

'Wild beasts won't eat me nor the sea drown me; what other conclusion can I draw?'

'The lion wasn't hungry and it was I that rescued you from the sea. Bullets will kill you for sure; besides, I think you are dying already.'

As if appearing on cue, thick, dark blood spilled from the corners of his mouth. He clapped his hand to his lips and the blood ran between his fingers and down his wrist. Mrs Green took a cloth and wiped it away. The boy brought the jars of paint and a jagged piece of mirror, which he laid down on the floor. Mrs Green took the boy's hand.

'It's best to leave a man and his wife alone at a time like this.'

The red paint was made from fat mixed with red clay, the white from fat mixed with chalk and the black from fat mixed with soot. He propped the mirror carefully against the wall and squatted before it, dipping his fingers in the various greases. A heavy slowness affected all his movements; he smeared black colour in clumsy patches round his eyes. She sat upright with her arms clasped around her knees, prim and grim with distaste.

'Did you go out last night looking for something to kill you?'

He did not reply so she knew it was true.

'What will you do if all this is real and you do, in fact, rescue Donally and you do, in fact, bring him home again?'

'He'll make me the Tiger Man,' said Jewel. In his eyes she thought she saw the birth of ambition. She said:

'If I took off your shirt, I think I would see that Adam had accepted the tattooed apple at last.'

'When I was asleep this morning, I dreamed I had been digging my own grave and woke up to find a lion kissing me. I was embraced by a lion last night. The lion, the king of beasts.'

He smeared red on his cheekbones.

'Am I beginning to look sufficiently terrifying?'

'Not to me.'

'Me neither. Perhaps I've lost the trick of it. I used to scare myself silly.'

'You've thrown away all your talismans and amulets, what will you do without them?'

'I shall find out soon how I manage, won't I?'

She saw his painted face in the mirror; dream and reality merged with such violence she laughed hysterically and repeated over and over again: 'You aren't yourself this morning, you aren't yourself this morning, you aren't yourself this morning.' When he finished painting, he drew his boots from a corner and put them on.

'You've omitted to tire your head.'

'Not today.'

'You are no longer a perfect savage, you are not paying sufficient attention to detail. You aren't in the least impressive; what will become of you?'

'I can hardly see,' he said. 'Kiss me before I go.'

'No!' she cried out, disgusted. 'Your mask has slipped too far for me to be able to respect you.'

'Kiss me.'

'Murderer,' she said. He swung round and lunged at her, falling heavily across her and striking her face. This time she hit him savagely in return and sent him sprawling on the floor.

'That's the third time,' she said with spiteful satisfaction. 'I warned you. Now you haven't a hope. You knew I'd be the death of you.'

He took some moments to regain his breath and then went off, reeling and unsteady of foot. She thought: 'I have destroyed him' and felt a warm sense of self-satisfaction, for quite dissolved was the marvellous, defiant construction of textures and colours she first glimpsed marauding her tranquil village; it had vanished as if an illusion which could not sustain itself in the white beams of the lighthouse. She got up and threw the pots of paint he left behind him into the weedy cleft between the station platforms. She threw the mirror after them, in case she saw his face in it, his former extraordinary face left behind there, for it must remain somewhere; she watched the mirror break with pleasure. She felt heavy and her breasts hurt. She went into the large room, once a waiting-room, and found Mrs Green cutting up meat. The cleaver slid slickly through the crimson hunk and she was nauseated.

'We can't go to the fishers today,' said Mrs Green. 'We'll stay here till Jewel comes back.'

'Do you think he'll come back?' asked Marianne, surprised.

'I dunno,' said Mrs Green and tears silently descended her withered cheeks. 'He should never have sent the Doctor away, he should have killed him outright and made a clean break. It was you that stopped him killing the Doctor, you wicked girl. It was you.'

Marianne drew herself upright and went out on to the platform. Jen sat there, dangling her feet over the edge.

'Why is your face all bruised?' she asked Marianne. 'Has Jewel begun to beat you?'

'Yes,' said Marianne.

'Then you'll be glad to see the last of him.'

'Yes,' said Marianne but then she found she, too, was crying. She walked down to the end of the platform, where the paving stones ended, and stared out across the shrubland. She made out the small company in the distance, five or six figures moving very slowly, walking the horses. They were no more than a mile away.

It was difficult to run for the sandy soil bristled thorns, thistles and sharp, dry, hard plants that tore her feet and even the grass was coarse and cut her. The day was grey as ashes. She felt a sharp pain in her side and stopped to rest for a moment but ran on again as soon as she could, for it was imperative. She ran until she could go no farther and they were still far ahead; she shouted as loudly as she could. Her voice cracked but carried clearly and Donally's son turned, she saw the flare of his scarlet coat. He must have spoken to Jewel for Jewel also turned his head and then looked quickly away. Until he handed the reins of his horse to Johnny, descended and walked slowly towards her, she inhabited a totally durationless present, a moment of time sharply dividing past from future and utterly distinct from both; she felt the sweat trickle down her backbone and the texture of each blade of grass and grain of earth beneath her feet.

She was seized with the most extreme happiness as she saw she could pull him towards her on an invisible thread and he entirely without volition of his own. But when he was near enough for her to see the blurred colours on his face, she also saw he was making the gesture against the evil eye. Suddenly she recognized it.

'They used to call that the sign of the Cross,' she said. 'It must be handed down among the Old Believers.'

'Did you call me back just to give me this piece of useless information?'

When he was close enough to touch, she ran her finger down his cheek and looked at the paint embedded under her fingernail.

'You see, I did not even love my brother much.'

He shied away, touched on the tenderest spot.

'And when I dreamed of the event, afterwards, which I did very often, it was only you that I remembered. It troubled me.'

He raised his eyes and they looked at one another with marvelling suspicion, like heavily disguised members of a conspiracy who have never learned the signals which would reveal themselves to one another, for to neither did it seem possible, nor even desirable, that the evidence of their senses was correct and each capable of finding in the other some clue to survival in this inimical world. Besides, he was so much changed, so far fallen from that magnificence bred of sophistication and lack of opportunity, and so was she, now in rags and haggard with sleeplessness and her condition, dirty also.

There was no sun to be seen today. When he returned to the posse, the small company of men diminished among the bare bushes until nothing more remained of them and she felt herself diminish with them, vanishing into the dangerous interior. When she could see him no more, she was surprised to find herself dislocated from and unfamiliar with her own body. Her hands and feet seemed strange extensions which hardly belonged to her; her eyes amorphous jellies. And she was not able to think.

She went off by herself down to the shore and searched for the place he had buried his rings but now the tide was high and lapped against the dunes themselves. The sea was brown in daylight, like an endless prairie, the colour of lions. She did not go as far as the lighthouse but watched the sea, which changed continually but always remained exactly the same. Far out, she once saw a fishing boat with a black sail but could make out no figures of men on board. She stayed out until it began to grow dark and could not think of anything, all day long. Mrs Green greeted her return inscrutably; she stirred a cauldron of stew with a huge metal spoon.

'I'll do that,' said Marianne. The old woman, interpreting her, surrendered the spoon with some bitter laughter.

'You'll not make him come back by getting his meal ready, you know,' she said. 'They call that sympathetic magic. And if he comes back, he'll bring the Doctor with him, more powerful than ever.'

She was already resigned, as was her custom. She was ready packed to make her own move, if necessary. Marianne went on stirring the stew. Jen and a crowd of children climbed on the station roof and looked out for the horsemen. Indoors, the cooking fire was reflected in a misty, cracked mirror on the wall; there also stood Marianne, unrecognizable to herself, leaning over the cauldron. Visions appeared in the steam, men, women and children with faces of horses and lions; the cicatrized man she had killed on the road made her a bow; her nurse's almost forgotten face grinned triumphantly for, in some sense, her prophecy had been fulfilled; finally, she there re-encountered her father, who merged imperceptibly with the image of the blind lighthouse and then disappeared in the slowly rising bubbles. Jen came tugging at her sleeve.

'I've seen them, I've seen them.'

'Is he with them?'

'It's too dark to make out.'

The food was almost cooked. She stirred the spoon round and at last Donally's son came in. The room was full of smoke, he materialized from it like an apparition in the pot. She thought he had painted himself red but it was blood with which he was covered from head to toe, naked to the waist for his coat was gone. He entered the room gingerly.

'Where are the others?' asked Mrs Green.

'Seeing to the horses.'

Marianne leaned over the fire and pinched a piece of meat. It was done.

'Is that Jewel's blood?' she asked the boy. He made a gulping, snivel- ling sound and whinnied in acquiescence. She fell down and the food spilled. The dogs fought over the meat swimming in gravy on the floor while Mrs Green helped her up and assisted her to the other room. She lay down again on the mattress where she would sleep alone in future.

'Go away,' she said but the boy stayed and lit a little lamp. Outside footsteps scurried about.

'I'll tell you what they're going to do, they're going to pack up and move on quick for the Soldiers are coming and Johnny says to leave you behind, for the Soldiers to get.'

'Oh, no,' she said. 'They won't get rid of me as easily as that. I shall stay here and frighten them so much they'll do every single thing I say.'

'What, will you be Queen?'

'I'll be the Tiger Lady and rule them with a rod of iron.'

After a pause, he went on: 'They split up to spy around and Jewel and me went straight into a nest of Soldiers, it was in a little wood. So they shot him in the stomach but then the others came and scared the Soldiers away but as for Jewel, it was all over with him.'

'How?'

'Quickly but painfully. Johnny and the others heard the noise and came whooping down.'

'Where was your father?'

'Nowhere to be seen.'

'So it was all fruitless or else it was a trap.'

'I don't know about that.' Radiant with intuition, he said: 'But I think they must have shot my father, I do think so.'

A little while later, he resumed: 'Oh, it was a horrid mess and Johnny and the others were like men possessed. There were only two Soldiers, Jewel and me were creeping through this little wood and it smelled of pine and the bullets came out of the forest and he fell down and the others came. I don't know if it was an ambush, even, or if they were just out shooting for pigeons, in the first place.'

'How do you come to be smothered in his blood?'

'He was writhing around and biting his lips to stop hisself making a noise, in case there were any more of them, and I held him, to keep him still, I suppose. Nobody else had time, he was swearing and cursing and they were scrabbling away at a hole ready to throw him into, but I held him and I felt him go. I was holding him and then he wasn't there any more, so I put pebbles on his eyelids to keep his eyes shut. And there was nothing no more.'

He seemed purely and strangely surprised at the swiftness and ease with which Jewel had departed from life; he looked at Marianne questioningly and giggled briefly. The ends of his hair had set in stiff spikes of dried blood.

'No more,' he said and relapsed into silence.